"You don't have to kiss me now, Gabe. Pete can't see what we're doing," Sandy murmured, her pulse still hammering from his embrace.

"I didn't kiss you to impress Pete," he said huskily.

"You know, if you keep up these kisses for four weeks, I might get addicted."

"I already am," he said, leaning closer.

"I hear warning sirens going off in my head," Sandy said softly. "Are we getting into deep water here?"

"I think we fell into an ocean the day we met."

"You felt it too—"

"You're sweet, Sandy, but sometimes you talk too much," he said firmly, pulling her closer to him.

"Who's talking?" she asked in a sultry tone, tilting her lips up to meet his. His tongue touched hers, and a flame licked along her veins, leaving a trail of heat throughout her body.

A long moment later he whispered, "Thank goodness for ginkgos. Otherwise I'd never have met you . . ."

WHAT ARE *LOVESWEPT* ROMANCES?

They are stories of true romance and touching emotion. We believe those two very important ingredients are constants in our highly sensual and very believable stories in the *LOVESWEPT* line. Our goal is to give you, the reader, stories of consistently high quality that may sometimes make you laugh, sometimes make you cry, but are always fresh and creative and contain many delightful surprises within their pages.

Most romance fans read an enormous number of books. Those they truly love, they keep. Others may be traded with friends and soon forgotten. We hope that each *LOVESWEPT* romance will be a treasure—a "keeper." We will always try to publish

LOVE STORIES YOU'LL NEVER FORGET
BY AUTHORS YOU'LL ALWAYS REMEMBER

The Editors

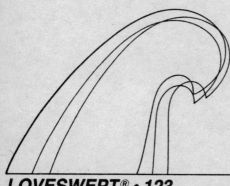

LOVESWEPT® • 123

Sara Orwig
Under the Ginkgo Tree

 BANTAM BOOKS
TORONTO • NEW YORK • LONDON • SYDNEY • AUCKLAND

UNDER THE GINKGO TREE
A Bantam Book / January 1986

ISBN 0-553-21740-2

Published simultaneously in the United States and Canada

Bantam Books are published by Bantam Books, Inc. Its trademark, consisting of the words "Bantam Books" and the portrayal of a rooster, is Registered in U.S. Patent and Trademark Office and in other countries. Marca Registrada. Bantam Books, Inc., 666 Fifth Avenue, New York, New York 10103.

PRINTED IN THE UNITED STATES OF AMERICA

O   0 9 8 7 6 5 4 3 2 1

Thanks, Norma, for your Christmas card . . .
Love to David, Susan, Joe, Anne, Chester.

One

Beneath a bright May sun, Saturday-morning traffic along the broad four-lane street moved briskly past a block-long nursery. Beyond its graveled parking lot stood an assortment of trees that partially blocked the view of a large metal building housing the office and cash register of London Garden and Nursery. Inside the office Gabe London sat behind a desk littered with papers. He rubbed the back of his neck and swore while he added a column of figures. His blunt fingers tangled in short locks of dark brown hair.

"Gabe, her ginkgos are wilted."

He looked up to see his younger brother, Pete, grinning at him from across the desk.

It took a second for Gabe to shift his thoughts from the figures in his head to his brother's joyful statement.

"Whose ginkgos have wilted?"

"The Casa Grande Senior Citizens' Retirement Center's," Pete said, brushing dirt off his jeans and shaking sun-bleached hair out of his eyes. His white T-shirt was dusty, the sleeves ripped off to reveal broad shoulders and brown arms bulging with muscles. "I'll take the truck out now to replace them, then stop on the way back to remove the Wilkens' pyracantha. See you at noon."

"Yeah." Gabe bent over the figures, adding quickly. As he looked at the column of numbers, the vision of his brother's happy face began to register. *Her* ginkgos. Something clicked, and Gabe dropped his pen. His blue eyes narrowed as he remembered the order for the ginkgos.

Shoving his chair away so rapidly it almost fell, he stood and yanked open a file drawer, riffling through papers.

"Pete!" He ran out of the office, hurrying past customers. His long, jean-clad legs stretched out, anger mounting with each step as he rushed past the long rows of flowers, the greenhouses, to the back of the graveled lot, just as the big truck was pulling away.

"Pete! Wait a minute!"

Pete braked and leaned out the window, a smile on his face.

Gabe sprinted to the truck. "This is the third set of ginkgos we've planted for Casa Grande."

"I know." Pete's smile broadened, and his voice held a dreamy quality.

"Dammit! We've never lost trees like that before. That's a big order. Mrs. Smith called Monday, mad as a wet hen over the first ones."

"Did she really? I missed her call."

Gabe's eyes narrowed, and he looked at the order, remembering when he had taken it. "Casa Grande Senior Citizens' Retirement Center," he read aloud. He had dealt with Derek Jackson when they planned the landscaping for the new center. He couldn't recall ever having seen Mrs. Smith.

"What's Mrs. Smith look like?"

Pete sobered and waved his hand. "Look like? Ah . . . an older woman. Gray hair, orthopedic shoes, hearing aid. I don't know. Bifocals . . ."

Gabe rubbed his jaw, looked at his twenty-one-year-old brother's wide blue eyes, and made a decision. "Yeah, I get the picture. You stay here."

"Hey!" Pete's grin faded instantly, and he blinked. "I can do this job!"

"Get out. I'll plant these trees for little ole Mrs. Smith. These damned ginkgos aren't going to wilt or shrink or lose their leaves."

"Hey, Gabe—"

"You and Tim stay right here."

"You can't do this by yourself," Pete protested while his fellow employee climbed out of the truck. "Tim can stay and I'll help you."

"Pete, I've been going over the monthly expenses. We need every penny. Do you know what these wilting trees are costing us? Get out of the truck. You man the cash register, and Tim can unload the shipment of cottonseed hulls."

Reluctantly, Pete stepped out. "You'll need my help."

"I'll manage," Gabe said grimly. He climbed inside, put the truck in gear, and looked at the order form to check the address. He shifted gears and the truck lumbered into the street, the ginkgos' leaves jiggling from the movement.

In the office of Casa Grande Senior Citizens' Retirement Center, Sandy Smith replaced the receiver of the phone and went down the hall to the apartment in which she lived. She stopped in front of the mirror, looking at herself, and had to laugh. Along with laughter was a degree of satisfaction. She still fit with ease into the cheerleader uniform she'd worn eleven years ago, in high school.

The phone rang, disturbing her thoughts, and she picked it up to hear her friend, Becky Conners, saying hello and then, "Just checking, Sandy. Do you want me to drive to the reunion?"

"I'll be glad to." Sandy twisted around and looked over her shoulder at the short green skirt, the white knit top, sneakers, and white ankle socks. "I feel ridiculous."

"I'll bet you don't look ridiculous."

"Don't bet too much." She tugged on one of her blond braids, which hung over her left shoulder.

"See you at half past ten. The picture-taking is at eleven sharp, then we'll have an assembly and lunch."

"I'll drive. I need to take some milk to Gran. There's the doorbell. Gotta run." Sandy hung up the phone and hurried to the door to open it.

Broad shoulders blocked out the light, and a blue knit shirt molded to a broad, muscular chest filled her view. A whiff of pine, the scent of a forest, assailed her, a tempting, faint odor that was inviting. Sandy looked up into clear, deep blue eyes fringed with thick, dark lashes, eyes that made her breathing stop—blue eyes that swiftly took in her cheerleading outfit. She blushed, aware of her silly appearance, but before she could say anything, the stranger snapped, "Is your mother home?"

Sandy ducked her head, feeling a thrill of satisfaction and amusement. Her twenty-ninth birthday approached, and she had been viewing it with trepidation. At the moment, to be mistaken for a high-school cheerleader by an attractive male was gratifying.

She couldn't risk speaking, afraid she would laugh, so she shook her head.

"I'm from London Nursery. Her ginkgos have wilted, and I've come to replace them."

"Oh, the ginkgo trees! This is the second time they've wilted."

"And the last time." As he looked around, she noticed he was so tall that his head almost touched the top of the doorway. Above a wide forehead, his wavy brown hair glinted with russet highlights. She inhaled deeply again, relishing the fresh scent. "Where are the ones that need replacing? Can you show me?"

"Sure. This way, Mr. . . . ."

"London, Gabe London," he said in a deep rumble that became imbedded in her mind.

"Hi. I'm Sandy Smith."

She closed the door to walk beside him, aware of his height and his long legs as they strolled down the wide, sloping lawn that led to the street. Behind them were rows of red brick apartments that were the heart of the senior citizens' center.

"Sandy, does your mother wear bifocals?"

"No, she doesn't." She glanced at him briefly, wondering what was on the man's mind. Of what interest could it be to Gabe London if Claire Jackson wore glasses?

He tilted his head to regard her. "Bifocals, orthopedic shoes," he mumbled. "I didn't realize your mother was young enough to have a daughter your age."

"Well, she is."

He looked down at her, assessing her in a manner that made her blush. "Sandy Smith. Were you here when the men from the nursery planted the ginkgos?"

"Yes, I was."

He nodded. "I don't think you'll have any more trouble with your ginkgos. You can tell your mother."

"You know what caused them to wilt?"

"I have an idea."

"What was it?"

"I'd call it 'Pete's Disease.' "

"A peat-moss disease?"

"That's close enough," he answered dryly.

She waved her hand. "There are the ginkgos. Those two are wilted, as well as one near the recreational center"—she paused and pointed toward a large red brick building—"and one to the east of my apartment. Just outside my bedroom window."

"Oh, swell." He walked up to one and touched a wilted leaf. The tree drooped; lovely fan-shaped leaves that had turned brown lay on the ground around the slender trunk. "Dammit!" Then, as if he remembered her presence, his head snapped around, and he said, "I'm sorry, Sandy."

She tried to remain solemn as she nodded. "That's all right."

His eyes narrowed. "Is something funny?"

"No, sir."

His glance raked over her impersonally, and he smiled. "You're a cheerleader for Wilson High."

"How'd you guess?"

He laughed. "School's out. Is this a summer cheerleading practice?"

"Something like that."

"I went to Wilson High too. Long before your

time. When will your mother be home? I'd like to talk with her about the ginkgos."

"She'll be away quite a while."

"Is your father here?"

"Nope, my stepfather's gone too."

"Your stepfather?"

"Derek Jackson."

"The owner. Well, I need to talk to your mom or step-dad about caring for the ginkgos."

"You can tell me."

He smiled. "I'll wait and tell your mother. Will you have her call when she gets in?" His hand squeezed into the tight pocket of his faded jeans. He produced a card and handed it to her. "There's my number."

"Mr. London, you'd better tell me. My parents are out of town. I'm managing Casa Grande."

"They left you in charge?"

"Well, I'm old enough!" She couldn't hold back her laughter this time, and it made him scowl.

"You're old enough, all right. Sandy, if you'll stay out of sight of my brother, Pete, I think the ginkgos will do fine."

She blinked. "You mean . . ." Her voice trailed off.

Picking a brown leaf off a branch he nodded solemnly. "I don't want to embarrass you, but I think the ginkgos are dying because Pete wants to come out to see you again."

"That's absurd! That kid—" She snapped off her words as Gabe London turned around to stare at her.

"He's twenty-one years old. Three or four years older than you are."

"Well, he looked young," she said solemnly.

"You tell him that the next time you see him."

"Yes, sir."

"Sandy, is something funny about this?"

"No, sir," she said, biting her lip to keep from laughing. Blue eyes were beginning to flash with pinpoints of fire, and she didn't want to become a target.

"You and Pete didn't plan this, did you?"

"Oh, no, sir! I'm the one who decided we'd plant ginkgos. I love the ginkgo tree. There's something magical about a ginkgo."

"It'll be magic if they survive."

"I want the ginkgos to live. It's discouraging to have them wilt like that. The folks here are interested in them, and it's distressing when the leaves turn brown and drop off."

"Distressing is putting it mildly," he muttered.

She glanced over the sweeping expanse of lawn with beds of purple and white periwinkles, lilacs, rose bushes, pink peonies, flocks of purple petunias along with young ginkgo, oak, and willow trees. "The landscaping is pretty. We've all been pleased with it."

"Thanks. Do you like the people here?"

"Oh, very much."

He smiled, a broad smile that made creases in his cheeks, that fanned crinkles from the corners of his eyes, and that threw invisible sparks into the air. "I don't mean to pry, but do you have a steady boyfriend?"

She looked down at the toes of her sneakers, a mixture of feelings coursing through her. The brown toes of his boots peeped out from under the frayed hems of his jeans.

He continued easily in his bass voice, which

claimed her total attention. "If you don't have a steady boyfriend, I might suggest to Pete that he give you a call, and end all this trouble with the ginkgos. He's older. Would your mother object to your going out with an older man?"

"I don't think it would work out."

"You're probably right. You're pretty mature, you know that?"

"Thank you. You really think so?"

"Yeah. I have to get my shovel from the truck. I should get the trees into the ground."

"You're going to do that by yourself? There were three men here before."

"I can manage."

She glanced at his broad shoulders, the bulging muscles in his arms, and silently agreed that he most likely could manage.

"Should the trees be watered daily?"

"Yep, for a time. We're heading into hot weather. Just lay the hose down by the roots and let it trickle in slowly. Do you take care of the trees?"

"Yes. Sometimes some of the residents help. Mr. Payton likes to putter around the yard."

He smiled warmly at her. "You're a nice kid, Sandy. I'll bet the folks here like having you around." He studied her. "Too bad you aren't just a year or two older."

"Don't wish that on me!" She was beginning to regret she hadn't told the truth from the first. Gabe London had the sexiest blue eyes she had ever seen and a voice that sent sparks dancing through her veins with every word. But it was too late now.

He laughed. "Look, have your mother give me a call when she gets back to town. I think the ginkgos will do fine now, but I'd like to talk to her."

"All right."

"It was nice to meet you, Sandy."

Something warmed inside. His voice was friendly, impersonal, but it had a furry depth, was masculine, and was unforgettable. Very unforgettable. She opened her mouth to tell him the truth about her age, then closed it. Ridiculous. He would plant the ginkgos and go, and their paths would never cross again. Shaking her head as if to clear away silly notions, Sandy extended her hand.

"It was nice to meet you, Mr. London."

His big hand enveloped hers, and a current ignited like sparks in a flaring match. She felt her cheeks grow warm. He frowned and peered intently at her, then shook his head as if coming out of a daze.

"I definitely know the cause of the ginkgos' wilting," he said softly, the raspy tone making her breath stop. He raised his voice to a normal level. "You have fun at practice." He turned away to go to his truck.

Sandy watched his brisk stride a moment before she returned to her apartment. For the first time—in how long?—she had noticed a man. Really noticed him. Maybe she was finally getting over Seth, something she had begun to think was impossible.

Rinsing dishes, she watched as Gabe London dug up one of the wilted ginkgos, tugging it out of the ground. Muscles strained in tanned arms, and his jeans molded to sinewy legs that were braced, feet apart, as he wrestled the tree. He ran his arm across his forehead and knelt down to cut open a bag of peat moss, each movement done with an athletic coordination, muscles flexing. Sandy sighed, leaned her hip against the kitchen counter, and continued to watch him work. After a time she filled a glass with ice water and went outside.

"Mr. London, would you like a drink?"

He straightened, leaning the shovel against his hip as he brushed muddy hands on his jeans and ran his forearm across his perspiring forehead again.

"Sure would. Thanks, Sandy." He accepted the glass, tilting his head back while he drained it. She looked at him standing beneath the ginkgo. The tree's slender young branches held long clusters of fan-shaped leaves that dangled above Gabe's thick brown hair. Leaves at the end of a branch lay on one broad shoulder. She had the notion that every time she looked at the ginkgo, she would remember him standing beneath it. Dirt smudged his cheek and the thighs of his jeans where he had rubbed his hands. He looked earthy, sensual, and appealing. She blinked and forced her attention to a nearby bed of petunias.

"Do you plan on going to college?"

She merely shrugged.

"You have any particular profession you would prefer?"

"I wish I were a physical therapist."

"Ah, that's commendable."

"I like people."

"And I'll bet they like you." He handed her the glass, and their fingers brushed lightly. "Thanks, Sandy."

"You're welcome."

He smiled, turned to dig, and she went back inside her apartment. She pressed her hand against her middle, realized what she was doing, and looked down at her fingers. What was there about Gabe London that made her instantly and totally aware of him? It wasn't mutual. His impersonal tone of voice made that clear. But even when it was impersonal, what a sexy voice! She peered out the window one more time.

As Sandy drove away, she waved, watching him wave back. She turned the corner, and her thoughts shifted to the problems before her. Gran. She thought of her stiff, unbending grandmother, Helen Crane, who had shared in raising her. Sandy sighed and worried over a new approach to get Gran to consider moving to Casa Grande. And every argument she mentally presented was an old one that Gran had already answered.

Gabe watched the car round the corner. Cute kid. Real cute. And acted older than her years. He had the most peculiar feeling that she was laughing at him, but there wasn't any basis for it. And for a moment there, when he had looked into her big green eyes . . .

He shook his head angrily and spaded a shovelful of red earth. He could cheerfully wring Pete's neck. Eight ginkgos originally, four replacements for wilted trees this time, three the last time—a total of fifteen ginkgos. Swearing softly, he thought of Pete's sappy grin and his dreamy "Her ginkgos are wilted." He'd like to wilt Pete. And he thought of the short skirt switching against her long, shapely legs as she walked away from him. "She's just a kid!" he ground out beneath his breath. Yet, she made him remember things forgotten—a feeling of lighthearted cheer that had been eluding him lately.

Angrily, Gabe pitched another shovelful of dirt aside and threw down his shovel to pull the tree out of the ground.

Two hours later, he sat in his office, staring at his brother. "I replaced each ginkgo. And these are going to thrive. Do you understand?"

"Why are you getting so hot under the collar? I can't help it if the ginkgos wilted."

"You can't?"

"Hell, no!" Pete's eyes grew round. "You think I did something to them?"

Gabe lowered his chair with a thud. "As a matter of fact, I met Sandy Smith. Why don't you just call her for a date and be done with it? Leave the ginkgos alone."

"Geez! You're suggesting I call her for a date?"

"Yeah, all she can do is say no."

"That's exactly what she did! I didn't think you'd approve."

"You've already asked her?"

Pete's face turned crimson. "Yeah."

"Pete, the world is full of cute girls."

"She's more than a cute girl!" His voice changed, and he stared into space. "When she smiles, it's beautiful. She has perfect teeth. White as snow."

Even though Gabe agreed about her smile, he snapped impatiently, "Will you forget Sandy Smith's smile? I'm trying to get this business rolling, and I can't afford to replace trees."

"Didn't you budget for replacements?"

"Sure, I did. But if this keeps happening, I'll run over the budget."

"You're not really going to run over the budget.

You've never run over a budget in your life, Gabe. She won't go out with me."

"Hell's bells. Look around."

"She has the prettiest smile in the U.S.A."

Gabe swore softly. "Will you get the wool out of your head!"

"Her eyes—they're as green as—"

"The leaves of a live ginkgo! She won't go out with you, so forget her."

"She prefers older men."

"Ha. Twenty-two?"

"I think your age. You didn't ask her out, did you?"

Gabe shoved a paper aside in disgust. "Pete, I have to get this bookkeeping done. No, I didn't ask Miss Sandy Smith out! That would be the day. I won't ask her out. I don't want to ask her out. She's a child."

"Some child! You've been working too hard, Gabe. Maybe something's happened to your system."

"Oh, for corn's sake! Will you go water the spirea?"

"When did you last have a date?"

"I don't remember." Hastily, he added, "I had a date last week with Joan."

"See, you couldn't even remember when it was. No business is that important."

"This one is."

"You just want to prove a point."

"Maybe I do. I know I don't want back in London and Holmes, doing accounting for Dad."

"Yeah. I want to play pro ball, and you know what Dad'll think of that."

"Pete, I have to get to work, and the spirea needs watering."

"I'm going. But, seriously, did you ever see such a smile? And her eyelashes—they have to be an inch long."

Gabe groaned and picked up a small packet of peat moss to toss at his brother. Pete ducked and jumped through the door, vanishing around the corner. Gabe stared at the paper in front of him and thought about Sandy Smith's smile. It was a lovely smile. He groaned aloud again. "Gabe, old man, you're going 'round the bend when you get to daydreaming about a kid!" He picked up a pen and concentrated on numbers, trying to forget Miss Sandy Smith.

Sandy climbed into bed, excited over the day's events, weary after the late hours at the reunion dance. It had been fun to renew old acquaintances. She stretched out, rubbing her cheek against the sheet, remembering faces that she hadn't seen for years. Remembering blue eyes and a smile that dazzled her right down to her toes. She blinked and stared at the ceiling. Gabe London. Why had he popped into mind?

She stirred and rolled over, and another face filled her thoughts. Seth Tarleton—the memory hurt, and the aching void didn't seem to change with time. Seth, whose velvety brown eyes twinkled when he laughed, whose deep-throated laughter always sent a tingle along her spine. Seth, who had said good-bye without a qualm and had gone to Washington to pursue a political career. She flounced on her back and closed her eyes tightly, willing sleep to come.

She heard something scrape. Sandy opened her eyes. Another scrape. A steady scrape, scrape. She sat up in bed, peering into the darkness, trying to place the noise.

Two

She threw back the covers and stepped out of bed, moving cautiously across the room.

Standing at the window, she pushed aside the curtain and peered out.

Someone was kneeling on the ground under the ginkgo tree. Something silver glinted in the moonlight as a man patted the dirt.

Remembering her conversation with Gabe London, Sandy became angry. She pushed open the window.

"Hey, you!"

The man rose to a crouching position and ran, dashing down the front lawn. Sandy switched on the outside light, rushed to yank open the front door, and heard the motor of a car fade into the distance. She gazed thoughtfully at the ginkgo tree before locking the door.

The next afternoon, she marched into the metal building at London Garden and Nursery. She paused, glancing around at the shelves holding bottles of insect spray, racks of flower seeds, stacks of clay pots on the earth floor, a long counter, and behind it a partition with a small sign reading,

"Office." Behind the counter she saw a brown head bent over papers. When she stopped in front of the counter, a fresh pine scent of summer woods assailed her. Momentarily disconcerted, she paused while she breathed deeply.

Gabe London worked behind the cash register. Out of the corner of his eye he'd seen someone enter the office, but he finished sacking the dahlia bulbs with his back to the counter.

"May I help you?" he asked, weighing the sack and closing it.

"Mr. London, my ginkgo has been tampered with!"

Startled, he turned, receiving a shock. His gaze went swiftly over the long blond hair caught up in a loose pile on top of her head, over the pale yellow knit shirt, down to the tight jeans she wore, and then back to her face. A faint scent of gardenia reached him. While she looked older than Sandy, the woman was too young to be Sandy's mother.

"Miss Smith?"

"That's right."

"Are you Sandy's sister?"

"No, I'm not! Last night I woke up and heard something scraping and scraping—"

"*Mrs*. Smith. Bifocals, orthopedic shoes, hearing aid. I might have known. . . ."

"Whatever are you talking about, Mr. London?"

"He said you wore all those."

"I don't know what you're talking about, nor do I care!"

"Are the ginkgos all right?"

"They were, as of nine o'clock this morning. As I was saying—"

"You are the youngest-looking mother to have a

high-school-age daughter I've ever seen." Awed, he stared openly at her.

She blinked, then focused intently on him. "You, and your brother, are nuts! Roasted nuts! Will you listen to me? I don't want those ginkgos to wilt again!"

"Oh, neither do I. You must have married when you were twelve."

She shook her head. "For your information, I've never been married."

"You haven't! I thought Sandy said her step-father—"

He stopped abruptly as her brows arched, and she laughed, her white teeth flashing. "I'm Sandy Smith."

"You're Sandy Smith?" He blinked. "As in pig-tails and cheerleader uniform?" Gabe stared at her. Her lashes must have been an inch long.

"A high-school reunion."

"Oh. I'll be damned." His gaze lowered over her high, small breasts, her narrow waist. The counter stopped his assessment, and he returned to green eyes that were beginning to flash with fire.

"Son of a gun! Why didn't you tell me! What an idiot I was!"

"I didn't say that!"

"You're laughing at me!" She ducked her head, and he felt both aggravated and amused.

"No, I'm not."

"And you were laughing yesterday! I thought you were, but . . . Damn, what an idiot I must have seemed."

"Actually, it was kind of fun."

They both smiled. Pete had good taste, all right. She did have a dazzling smile that made him want to grin in return. And her eyelashes were every bit an inch long. Such big green eyes. He wanted to reach across the counter and touch her.

"My ginkgo," she said softly with a hint of laughter still in her voice.

His mind began to go back over his conversation with Pete. "What about your ginkgo?"

"Last night I scared someone away who was digging beneath one of the ginkgos."

"Oh, no!" Gabe exclaimed. "He promised me!"

"Be that as it may. I don't want these ginkgos to wilt."

"Neither do I."

"You control your brother. I will not go out with him on a date. I'm too old for him."

"How much too old?" Gabe held his breath.

"Mr. London!"

"C'mon, Sandy. It's Gabe. How much too old?"

"That's neither here nor there. Tell him to leave my ginkgos alone!"

"I'll do that. Twenty- . . . five?"

"Twenty-eight for a few more weeks."

"Nice!"

"Don't start on me."

He laughed. "Don't worry. I date a cute little redhead. I want the ginkgos to live, and I'm a busy man. But I can understand Pete's obsession."

She smiled, full red lips parting over even white teeth, and he thought that smile alone should be enough to revive the ginkgos. "Isn't there a regular guy? Someone you can flaunt in Pete's face?"

"Unfortunately, no," she answered, waving a hand with slender fingers devoid of rings. "I'm busy too."

"You're the manager of Casa Grande?"

"Yes. It's in the family. My stepfather owns it, and I'm running it while he opens two more complexes for senior citizens in Texas. I keep things going smoothly, drive the bus three times a week, keep books, oversee the landscaping, do little odds and ends for the residents."

"Gabe, where are the dwarf crape myrtles?" Pete called as he rolled a wheelbarrow down the aisle. "I need— Holy smoke! Sandy!"

"Hey! Pete!" Gabe yelled.

Too late, Pete looked down as Sandy shrieked and pressed against the counter. The wheelbarrow lurched and slammed into a stack of clay pots, breaking the clay and sending pots tumbling down. Sandy stepped out of the way.

"Gee whiz! I'm sorry. Are you hurt? Let me get the clay off your feet."

"You stay away from my feet!" She jumped back, landing squarely against Gabe, who had come around the counter.

"Oh!" Sandy exclaimed, stepping on Gabe's toes. His arms went around her in a reflex action, and he felt the softness of her, her tiny waist, the faint whiff of gardenia stronger now.

"You two!" She stepped out of Gabe's arms and glared at them angrily.

"I didn't do anything," Gabe said. "You backed into me."

"My ginkgos better live. Now the petunias look as if they have the blight."

"Pete, if you don't—"

"I'm getting this up as fast as I can."

"I'll come out to look at your petunias," Gabe said.

"And when you do, please keep away from me!"

Sandy turned abruptly and left, climbing into a red car to drive away, a flurry of dust hanging in her wake.

Gabe looked at his brother, who worked swiftly, picking up bits of clay. "Were you out there last night, doing something to the ginkgos?"

"Think I'm some kind of nut? Why would I do that?"

"I won't answer that one." Gabe saw a customer standing nearby and went to wait on her.

An hour later he stood on the lawn of Casa Grande, his anger mounting as he surveyed the beds of drooping petunias. He knocked on the door, and when Sandy Smith opened it, he gazed into wide green eyes that caused a change in his pulse rate. Her hair cascaded down her back, the ends curling under softly. Trying to hide his reaction, he kept his voice matter-of-fact as he said, "Hi. I came to see about the trees and the flowers. Will you tell me again about last night?"

She leaned one hip against the door, shook blond hair away from her face, and said, "I was in bed and heard something scraping."

For an instant Gabe conjured up a vision of Sandy stretched in bed, her silky hair fanned over a pillow, and he didn't hear a word she said. He tried to pay attention.

"I yelled at the man and he ran off. When I got to the door, I heard a car driving away."

"I can't afford to keep replacing ginkgos." He fought an urge to pick up long strands of golden hair that lay on her shoulders.

"It seems to me you should make that announcement to Pete."

"I have, and it didn't mean a thing. Money's relative to him. He's in college on a shoestring. I have my own business, my apartment, my car. He thinks I own the world." Gabe found it difficult to keep his attention on their discussion. Her lips were full, rosy, and inviting. "Bills don't mean much to him. Maybe you should try another nursery."

"You're kidding!" She put her fists on her hips. "You guaranteed those trees. I can't get another nursery now. You should've warned me about your weird brother when I ordered the trees. I didn't know he came with the ginkgos."

"He's not weird. Well, not real weird. He hasn't done anything like this before," Gabe said, but for an instant he was sympathetic with Pete. "Actually, he's popular, and girls call him."

"Then why doesn't he go out with them?"

"He has a regular girl—or, rather, he had one. She was tall, blond, hazel eyes. There's a resemblance of sorts. But she's gone for the summer."

"Can we send for her to come home?"

He laughed. "Unfortunately, no. Kim's on an art tour of European cathedrals, and they had a fight before she left. She won't be home for two months, and then she's going to meet her parents in New York and stay there for another two weeks."

"Why me?" Sandy muttered.

"Let me stay here tonight and watch for him."

"Oh!" She backed up a step and pulled the door slightly closed. "What is this? *Two* weirdos?"

"No, I just want to catch Pete working on the ginkgos."

"Then hide in the lilac bushes and wait for him." Stepping outside, she waved her hand. "Look at the petunias. They're turning gray. He's ruining everything."

Gabe turned to look at the beds of drooping flowers. He ran his fingers through his hair. "We'll replace them, and I won't let Pete near this place."

"That's good news."

"All right, I'll come out and hide in the lilacs tonight, but don't turn me in for a prowler. And where can I leave my car?"

"I'll show you." As they walked around her apartment, he was aware that her head was at the height of his shoulder. Beyond Sandy's yard was a street that curved between two rows of red brick apartments. At the end of the row was a large building.

Gabe paused to survey everything. "The trees back here look fine."

"They do." She touched his arm lightly, yet he could feel the contact as if a brand burned his skin. She moved her hand away, and he heard a swift intake of her breath, making him wonder if she had the same reaction he did. Her voice was slightly lower as she said, "You can leave your car down there, by Apartment Fifteen. It's the last one before our apartment building and the infirmary. Mr. Payton doesn't drive. I'll tell him you'll be parking there." She tilted her head. "You'll really hide in the lilacs?"

"What a way to spend the evening!" He grinned, and his heart skipped faster when she grinned in return.

That night as he shifted his weight, he wished he had pushed harder to stay inside with her. The ground was damp, and it was boring to sit in a bush that sent little leaves slithering down the back of his neck with every movement. Of all the goofy things to be doing. He had books to balance, orders to type up, he hadn't called Joan in a week, and he hadn't returned his father's call today. Gabe rubbed the back of his neck. He would like to plant his fist squarely on Pete's jaw. And no one had come near a ginkgo.

"Psst!"

He glanced around. A door was ajar, a wisp of white moving slightly in the darkness. "Come inside," came a hoarse whisper.

"I thought you'd never ask."

He moved quietly inside, his eyes well adjusted to the darkness.

Sandy pulled her robe closer beneath her chin. "I felt sorry for you out there. You want to wait inside?"

"Do I ever!"

"Are you sure your brother doesn't know you're here?"

"Positive. Are you sure someone was digging beneath a ginkgo the other night?"

"Absolutely! You think I made that up? You can—"

"Hey, calm down," he said. "I'm teasing. I believe you. Where can I sit to see the ginkgo?"

Her cheeks turned pink as she answered. "My bedroom. Can you see if I don't turn on a light?"

"My eyes adjusted to the darkness two hours ago," he said as he took in her high-necked white cotton robe, her hair tumbling free. His mind reveled in imagining how soft she would feel in his arms.

As he followed Sandy, her long hair swayed with each step. It fell in a curtain of gold to hang to her waist, and again he had to curb a compelling urge to reach out and wind his fingers in it.

He shook his head and followed her into a small bedroom, where the covers were turned down and rumpled on the bed. She stopped in the moonlight, and he saw the pink deepen in her cheeks.

"I didn't know I'd have company."

"Thanks for rescuing me. This is a lot better than under the lilacs. I think I have leaves down my back."

She smiled and waved her hand toward the window. "There's the ginkgo."

Gabe sat down on a cedar chest in the shadows near the window. "Going to join me?" he asked, trying to keep amusement out of his voice as he saw her eyes widen, guessing she must just now have thought about what she would do while he was in her bedroom.

She frowned and sat in a rocker, which was in the moonlight. She smoothed her robe over her knees, tightened it beneath her chin, and shook her hair away from her face. It swirled across her shoulders, moonbeams catching golden highlights as long strands settled.

"Is your brother always this weird?"

"No. He's had the usual crushes, more than the usual number of girlfriends. I think it's your long eyelashes."

"Good grief! I'd hate to trim them."

"Yeah, don't do that! They're perfect."

"Thank you."

"It's either your long lashes or your big green eyes—"

"Will you stop!"

"I'm just telling you what Pete said. I wish he'd show up and I could catch him. It would put an end to all this foolishness. Why are you stuck with this job?"

"I'm not stuck."

"Okay. I'll phrase it another way. What are you hiding from?"

"I wish you were back under the lilac."

"My question scares you?"

"No, it implies things that aren't true. I like working with people. Why do you have a nursery?"

He smiled in the darkness, sure that she wasn't half so interested in his life as she was trying to prevent his asking questions about hers. "I like the outdoors. I like working with growing things. I want to run my own business, be outside."

"I don't remember the London Nursery being there long ago. Is it fairly new?"

"I started about sixteen months ago. Before that, I was an accountant in practice with my father."

"Oh. London and Holmes?"

"You've heard of them?"

"Who hasn't in this part of the country? That's quite a change. Did you go with your father's blessing?"

"No, I didn't," Gabe answered frankly, surprised at her question. "He's bitter about it, and he expects me to fail."

"Why would he think you'd fail if he expects you to succeed when you work with him?"

"He hopes the nursery will fold and I'll return to accounting. It's the first time we've really been at cross-purposes." He ran his hands through his hair, short locks of brown hair springing back into waves. "You're easy to talk to, Sandy Smith."

"Thanks. That's what the folks here tell me. Haven't you talked about your career with the cute redhead?"

"Joan? No, she's not interested in hearing about business. We never discuss it." He leaned forward. "Do you mind if I open the window a fraction and unlatch the screen? Then, if Pete comes, I can step out and catch him. The day hasn't arrived yet when he can outrun me."

"Go ahead," Sandy said, watching moonlight glint on his dark hair. His broad shoulders were silhouetted against the window.

"If he shows up, do you have an outside light you can turn on?"

"Yes, I'll switch it on if you go after him."

As he sat down, she asked, "Do you have other brothers and sisters?"

"Yes, a sister who's younger."

"She doesn't work at the nursery?"

"No, Jeanie's an accountant in my father's firm. And she likes working there, thank goodness." He shifted his long legs, stretching them out near Sandy's ankles. She glanced down momentarily.

"Seems as if one offspring in the business would be enough."

"Not for my father. We were always close when I was growing up. I think I did a lot of the same things he did when he was young. Football, that type of thing. From the time I was born he expected me to go to work for him."

"Oh, look!" Sandy touched his knee, and the contact all but sizzled, making him forget what she had said. "There he is!"

Three

He turned and stiffened as he watched a shadow separate from the darkness at the corner of the garage. A man was crouched over; he pranced on his toes to the ginkgo, where he knelt down and placed the bags he held in each hand on the ground. He also had a trowel.

"Hot damn!" Instantly Gabe stepped through the window. His foot came down on a stick that snapped. The man stood up and started to run. Gabe sprinted to him, caught his shoulder, and hauled back his fist.

"Got you! So help me, Pete!"

"Hey, let me go!" the man yelled, while nearby a woman screamed.

Lights came on, shedding a yellow brilliance over the dark grounds. Gabe stopped, his fist poised in the air, inches short of striking a quivering little man with tufts of white hair on his head and spectacles awry on his face.

As Gabe stopped, the man yelled, "Mrs. Fenster! Help!"

Something came down on Gabe's head with a clang. Pain shot down his neck, his spine, and he saw stars for an instant, before the world faded into blackness as he dropped to the ground.

He regained consciousness with his head cradled in a warm, soft lap. Someone was a hazy blur above him; dimly he heard voices. An angel was over him, his head in her lap. Her lips were red, her golden hair falling over him. He reached up and wrapped his arm around her neck to pull her down.

"Joan, love . . ." He slurred the words.

She yelped and wriggled and struggled against him, but he wanted to hold her. He tightened his arm, pulling her closer. "Don't get . . . to kiss . . . angel often," he mumbled. His lips touched hers briefly. She was so sweet. . . .

He was dumped on the cold, hard ground, jarring his throbbing head. He blinked and sat up, everything clearing as he looked around and remembered what had happened.

"Sandy!"

"You stop, or Mrs. Fenster will flatten you with the trowel again!"

"Mrs. Fenster?" He rubbed the back of his head and looked at the three people standing over him. Sandy Smith stood with her hands on her hips, her face flushed. Beside her were two other people, a small man with white hair and trifocals, and a stout lady who wore a yellow robe, fuzzy yellow slippers, and a nightcap. And carried a trowel.

"What happened?" Gabe asked, rubbing a knot on his head. "Is this who's been killing the ginkgos?"

"Meet Mr. Payton and Mrs. Fenster." Sandy raised her voice. "This is Gabe London, of London Garden and Nursery."

"How'd do?" Mr. Payton said. Cautiously he offered his hand, while Mrs. Fenster nodded. "I wasn't harming the tree," he explained. "I knew how worried Sandy was about it, so I was trying to take care of it. I wanted to put my own plant food on it."

"Couldn't you have told Sandy and worked on the tree in the daytime?"

"How's that?" Mr. Payton asked, and Gabe raised his voice, repeating his question.

"Sorry, I don't hear too well. Yes, I could, but I didn't want her to think we were worried unduly about the tree. I meant to come out early this evening, but I dozed off."

"I wondered what had happened to him," Mrs. Fenster said. "I called and woke him up. Young man, I'm terribly sorry I hit you with the trowel. I saw you grab Mr. Payton."

"I understand," he said, and glared at Sandy. She shrugged her shoulders. He held his head and stood up, swaying slightly. Immediately Sandy slipped her arm around his waist. He smelled something as sweet as gardenias and leaned closer.

"Are you all right?" she asked. "We have a nurse here."

"I'll be all right if I can just sit down in a chair and have a drink of water."

"I'm terribly sorry," Mrs. Fenster said again.

"Think nothing of it. I'm sorry I almost struck Mr. Payton," Gabe said loudly.

"So am I!" Mr. Payton exclaimed. "Goodness, next time, Sandy, I'll tell you before I work on the tree. I didn't know your boyfriend would be watching. . . ."

"He's not my boyfriend, Mr. Payton! He's from the London Nursery."

"How's that?"

Mrs. Fenster shouted, "He's not her boyfriend! He's from a nursery."

"Runs a nursery!" Mr. Payton said, and shook Gabe's hand.

Gabe's head hurt, he didn't feel like shouting at Mr. Payton, and Sandy smelled so nice. He leaned a little more heavily on her and groaned. Her arm tightened around his waist.

"Let's get you inside. 'Night Mr. Payton, Mrs. Fenster."

After shouted good nights, they parted. Gabe held Sandy close, remembering the softness of her lips beneath his. How soft she was, how special that brief touch had been—and how badly it made him want more. He glanced down at her, and his fingers squeezed more tightly, feeling her warm flesh beneath the robe.

She closed the door behind them and led him into the living room.

"Lie down on the sofa and I'll get you a drink of water." They reached the sofa and he sat down, moving deftly to pull her off-balance so she sat down in his lap.

"Hey!" Sandy looked into wide blue eyes.

"I remember a brief kiss out there," Gabe said, lowering his voice.

A tingle slithered down Sandy's spine. He was so close, his blue eyes focused on her lips. And she remembered too. It had been the slightest touch of their lips, but she had felt it to her heart.

"I'll get your drink of water," she said with all the firmness of melting snow.

He placed his hand behind her head, barely holding her. "In a minute. First, there's something more urgent." His voice was fuzzy and deep, his breath fanned her face lightly, and he leaned closer with each word until their lips met.

The contact brought the roar of gale winds to Sandy's ears, yet there wasn't a sound in the room except for the pounding of her heart. Again his lips brushed hers in a feathery caress, then slowly moved over hers, pressing, rubbing against them, and she parted her lips.

Gabe settled her against his shoulder, tightened his arm around her waist, and kissed her. His tongue touched hers in a tentative searching. Sandy closed her eyes, then opened them wide in shock. Her heartbeat skittered. She had tightened her arms around Gabe's neck, and she discovered something.

She leaned back a fraction to look intently at him.

"My goodness!"

"I'd hoped for a better reaction than that. Something that would match mine."

"Oh, you should be flattered," she whispered.

He toyed with a strand of golden hair, pushing it back and tracing the curve of her ear. "How's that?"

"I've been in love, and he's gone, but he gets in the way every time. Usually so much in the way, I don't like anyone else's kisses." She looked into blue eyes that made her temperature jump.

"And?"

"That didn't happen this time."

"Are you sure?" he asked solemnly.

"Very. It's the most amazing thing. You can't imagine how terrible it's been."

"Let's make certain." He leaned down to kiss her again, and it was all and more than it had been before. His arms crushed her to his hard chest, his tongue probed deeply into her mouth, and he shifted, leaning down with her head on the sofa pillows.

A hot ache began in her loins, spreading upward, to make her moan softly. She forgot everything, relishing Gabe's kisses, until he raised his head.

"Is he in the way?"

"Who?"

He came down again, kissing her deeply, but the interlude had served to restore her wits. She pushed and wriggled away to stand up.

"My goodness! What a night this has been. Let me get your drink."

She returned in a moment to stand at arm's length and hold out a glass of ice water. As he accepted it, his eyes sparkled with amusement.

"Are you sure you don't need to visit the nurse?"

"No, but will you look and see if I'm bleeding?"

"No kisses, now."

"The kisses were bad?"

"We hardly know each other. And I had a definite reaction to you."

"Good. I had a definite reaction to you," he said warmly.

"Let me look at your head."

He turned around, and she moved closer. Touching him lightly, she gasped. "What a knot!"

"Is it bleeding?"

"No."

"Well, I can talk coherently, so I guess I'll survive. Why didn't Mrs. Fenster get Pete with her trowel?"

"I'm so sorry you got hurt."

He turned around, drank the water, and set the glass on a coaster. "I might as well give up and go home. And I'm not going through this every night."

"Thanks for trying."

"I have an appointment with a client Monday to go over landscape plans, so I'll have to send Pete out to replace the petunias."

"That's all right. I drive the van Monday, so I won't be here too much of the time."

"Where do you go?"

"I take residents to Delmar Shopping Center and wait while they shop. Sometimes I push Mrs. Kelsy around, because she's in a wheelchair. After two hours, everyone gets in the van and we come back here."

"You're young to spend your time that way."

"It's a nice way to spend my time." She wrinkled her nose at him. "It's better than sitting in an office adding little figures."

"Who is he?"

"Who?"

"The guy you can't forget."

She shrugged. "Just a guy who used to live here and lives in Washington D.C. now."

"Were you engaged?"

She nodded. "I'm sorry I mentioned him."

"Oh, no. Under the circumstances, I need to know these things."

"What circumstances?"

He placed his hands on her shoulders, pushing long strands of hair back out of his way. His fingers trailed lightly back and forth beneath her ears, starting little sparks of awareness.

"I think you and I are going to get to know each other well," he said softly in his rumbly, sexy voice.

It was difficult to talk, but she tried. "I thought you dated a cute redhead named Joan, that you're busy, and that you—"

"My big mouth. I think the priorities got shuffled tonight."

She smiled and ran her finger down his cheek. "Tempting, but no."

"Any reasons?"

"I have my hands full here. And while I had a reaction to you, I'm really not ready to get involved."

"We won't get involved. We'll just be friends." He stepped back and smiled, offering his hand. "How's that? Just friends?"

She took his hand, shook it, and smiled, answering, "That would be very nice." But somewhere deep inside, she had a suspicion he didn't mean a word he was saying.

Monday came and went. Gabe took care of his business, and only thought of Sandy occasionally. Tuesday, he was stacking clay pots in front of the building, when a car whipped into the lot and a door slammed. He lifted two big pots from the wheelbarrow.

"There you are!"

He looked up to see Sandy Smith with her hands on her hips, her green eyes flashing. She wore a violet sundress and had her hair tied behind her neck.

One glance at her expression and he envisioned wilted ginkgos. "Morning," he said as he pulled off dusty gloves. "Some ginkgos have curled up their leaves, I suppose."

"The ginkgos are fine. The new petunias are glorious. The periwinkles have grown an inch."

"But you're madder than a poked hornet. What's happened?"

"I wish I'd never heard of London Nursery. The periwinkles and petunias have been trimmed. They spell 'I love Sandy Smith'!"

"Oh, no."

"Oh, that's not all."

He felt hot anger start in the pit of his stomach and come burning up into his cheeks. "What else?"

"There are periwinkles planted in little clumps of hearts. And he has called me three times to ask me for a date!"

"Are you going out with him?"

"Oh! How can you ask something like that?"

"How am I to know what you told Pete?"

"It wouldn't bear repeating. Do something about him!"

"I will," he said, looking at her lips and remembering her kisses.

"And will you do something about my periwinkles? I don't want 'I love Sandy' growing larger and larger as the summer progresses. Last night it was embarrassing to explain to my date why the periwinkles spelled out 'I love Sandy.' "

"The guy is home from Washington D.C.?"

"No. I go out on dates with other men."

"Oh. Friend basis or otherwise?"

"Friends. They just don't—" She bit her lip.

"That's not important. Will you replace my periwinkles?"

"Yes. I'll do it today. They don't what? What did you say?"

She blushed and shook her head. "Never mind."

He tilted his head to one side and smiled, beginning to enjoy himself. "You're blushing. Other men just don't do what that makes you blush?"

"There are moments you're as annoying as Pete."

"I'm just asking you a question."

"Have you heard of politely dropping something when someone doesn't want to talk about it?"

"What don't you want to talk about?" he persisted. "The men you date just don't—"

"Mean anything to me. We're friends."

"That isn't what you started to say. Why would that make you blush?"

"They don't kiss like you do. There. Satisfied?"

He grinned, feeling a glow inside. The day had just improved considerably. The sun shone a little more brightly. "It's great for starters. Thank you."

"That isn't why I came."

"Don't say it. Leave me in bliss."

"You sound like your brother."

"I hope not," he said, the worry and aggravation returning. "I don't know what's gotten into Pete. He's never been this way before."

"Just keep him away from me and Casa Grande." She tilted her head to one side. "He said you told him to ask me out."

"For corn's sake. I told him that after the first time I saw you, when I thought you were in high school."

"You're sure?"

"Yes. He's too young and too immature for you."

"Thank you for that."

"While I, on the other hand—"

She waved her fingers. "Stop. I think it's best if I don't get to know your family any better. How's your head? Mrs. Fenster wanted to know."

"A little sore, that's all." A horn blared, and someone waved frantically from a big red truck.

"There's Pete now."

"I'm going."

The truck turned the corner and disappeared, going toward the back of the nursery.

"I'll replace the periwinkles."

She reached for her car door. "Just keep your brother away from Casa Grande!" She climbed in, slammed the door, and drove off as Pete came running from the back.

"Sandy, hey, wait!"

She drove into the street and was out of sight. Gabe faced Pete and tried to control his temper. "Dammit!"

"Something wrong?"

"Yes, something's wrong. Her periwinkles spell 'I love Sandy.' "

"I know." Pete grinned. "Did you ever see such skin? So smooth and tan, and that long golden hair—"

"Do you want a summer job?"

"No, I have one."

"Do you want to keep the one you have?"

"Sure."

"Then you're not to plant one more flower at Casa Grande. You leave Casa Grande to me."

"Oh, you finally noticed her! Have you got a date with her?"

"No, I don't. She's in love with some guy in Washington."

"A senator."

"Senator?" Gabe was startled.

"Yeah. Oklahoma's youngest senator. Senator Tarleton."

"Is that the man she dated? How'd you know?"

"One of the men at the retirement center told me. Mr. Payton. He said Mrs. Fenster hit you over the head with a trowel."

"Yes, she did," Gabe answered, thinking about Sandy and Senator Tarleton. He remembered meeting Tarleton briefly at a dinner two years ago. He liked Seth Tarleton and had voted for him in the election. The man was handsome, with a winning, easygoing manner. Gabe's thoughts were interrupted by Pete.

"How come Mrs. Fenster hit you? Were you trimming up the periwinkles too?"

"No! I was out there watching for you."

"You don't say. Mr. Payton said it was almost midnight. That's a silly time to be watching for me. If you wanted me, why didn't you just call? Have you noticed her fingers?"

"Listen here. I'll fire you. F-I-R-E you if you take any more orders out to Casa Grande, if you touch the periwinkles or petunias or ginkgos. Tim and I will do the work there. Do you understand?"

"Okay. Shall I unload the truck now or deliver the crepe myrtles for the Hornbecks?"

"How come you accepted my orders so easily?"

"You're the boss."

"Yeah. Deliver the crepe myrtles. Tim and I'll unload the truck. Patsy will wait on the customers." Gabe thought about the female employee he had hired to sell plants to the customers. "Have you ever thought about asking Patsy for a date? She's cute."

"Patsy? Patsy doesn't have long legs, gorgeous eyelashes, golden hair, and pink cheeks. I'll bet I can circle Sandy's waist with my hands."

"I'll bet you'd better not try."

"She has the tiniest waist. Don't tell me you haven't noticed her waist!"

Gabe could remember exactly how it felt to have his arm around Sandy's tiny waist. "Well, maybe I did."

"Maybe?"

"Will you start thinking about crepe myrtles! Sandy Smith is just another female," Gabe said firmly, but he could also remember her kisses with total clarity.

"You lead a dull life."

"My life is fine. Are you forgetting Joan? And Sandy Smith is too old for you."

"Bull. That's old-fashioned."

"She's too mature. That isn't old-fashioned. It's the bald truth."

"I'm mature."

"It was really mature to prune the periwinkles to read, 'I love Sandy.' Now, will you get to work?"

"Sure thing. Twenty inches. I'll bet her waist is just twenty inches around. And she has straight white teeth. And her kisses . . . zowie!"

Two flowerpots fell from Gabe's hands and cracked into bits at his feet. "You've kissed her?"

Pete smiled, gazing into space. "Yeah!"

"When did you get chummy enough with her to kiss her?" He hated prying into his brother's activities, but he couldn't keep from asking, and a slow burn ignited.

Pete's face flushed. "I grabbed her when she wasn't expecting it."

The burn faded instantly. "Did it ever occur to you that you might have a problem?"

"Constantly. And her initials are S.S."

"Crepe myrtles!"

"Okay, okay!" Pete left, and Gabe continued unloading the wheelbarrow, stacking clay pots neatly, but all he could see was Sandy Smith. Her waist probably was twenty inches around. And her teeth were white and straight. And she smelled like gardenias again today. And he couldn't just reach out and grab her, but he understood why Pete wanted to. Her kisses were zowie. He shook his head, set his jaw, and tried to think about clay pots.

A week passed, and Gabe was beginning to forget about Pete and Casa Grande. Tuesday morning he drove to work, placed an order for a shipment of chrysanthemums, and settled in the office to go over the books before they opened the nursery for customers. When the phone rang, he reached for it without looking at it. "London Garden and Nursery."

"Come get your brother!"

"Hello?"

"Gabe London?"

"Sandy Smith. Oh, no. I told Pete he wasn't to work out there again."

"He's peeping in my kitchen window, because I won't answer the door. Come get him."

"If you'll let him inside to talk to me, I'll—"

"No! I hate to tell you, but there's a side to your brother you don't know. He's all hands, and I won't unbolt the door."

"I'll come remove him. Or you can get Mrs. Fenster and her trowel."

"And now there's a little old lady peeping in the kitchen window with him."

"One of your people?"

"No, I've never seen her before. She has big gold earrings and long fake eyelashes and gray hair combed into a bun on top of her head. She's wearing a silver star on top the bun and holding a yellow cat."

"Sandy, I'm coming. That's my grandmother!"

Four

Sandy heard a click. She slammed down the receiver and peered around the corner at the kitchen window. Gabe London's grandmother smiled and waved, motioning Sandy to go to the door.

Sandy took a deep breath, causing her white shirt to pull tautly over her breasts. She squared her shoulders, went to the back door, and hooked the screen.

"Morning, Sandy," Pete said with a smile, trying to open the screen door. "This is my grandmother, Dorina London."

"How do you do, Mrs. London." Sandy stared at a small woman who wore high black heels, tight leather pants, a bright pink shirt, and held a fat yellow cat.

Dorina smiled. "I'd like to look at the apartments, if I may."

"Dodo's thinking about moving out here," Pete said happily.

Sandy felt a knot form in the pit of her stomach. "I'll get a key." She pulled down the key ring. Last Friday she hadn't made the connection when she took a call from Mrs. Walter London, who was interested in Casa Grande. There were still two apartments vacant, and Sandy had given Mrs. London the information about the Center. Grimly now, she stepped outside.

"What lovely hair you have," Mrs. London said.

"Yeah!" Pete smiled.

"Thank you," Sandy said to Mrs. London.

"After talking to you, Miss Smith, I think this is just what I want. And you said I could keep Pookums here."

"Yes, we allow small pets. No large dogs."

"Oh, I don't have a large dog. Poor Pookums couldn't stand a large dog."

Sandy sidestepped Pete, placing Mrs. London between them. "The two-bedroom apartment you were interested in is in the red brick building across the street." With each word her voice dropped. The apartment was only yards away, across the narrow asphalt street.

Behind them a car door slammed, but Sandy was too worried about the turn of events to consider it. She paused on the porch of the apartment, feeling a knot of anger mushroom and grow. First the trees and flowers, and now Pete London wanted to move his grandmother to Casa Grande! She reached to unlock the door, and dropped the key. Instantly, Pete retrieved it and held it out to her. As she took it, his big hand closed over hers.

"I think Dodo will like it here better than living alone. I would."

She struggled to free her hand. "Mrs. London, will you tell your grandson to release my hand?"

"Let go of her hand," a deep voice said, "or I'll deck you!"

"Gabe!" Pete jumped away. "I'm not here for the nursery! I'm here with Dodo."

Sandy turned to see Gabe striding up, and her heart jumped. The wind blew locks of his wavy hair away from his face. He was dressed in old jeans and a sleeveless knit shirt that revealed muscles as developed as Pete's. Yet, in spite of Gabe's casual appearance, he had a commanding, take-charge manner. "Dodo, why are you and Pete here?"

"Gabel, don't shout at Dodo. You know it gets me flustered, and poor little Pookums can't bear to hear a gruff voice."

"Why are they here?" Gabe looked at Sandy.

She met his eyes, and for a full twenty seconds she forgot her anger. His eyes were as blue as she had remembered. He arched his brows, smiled, and she remembered his question. "Your grandmother is considering becoming a resident."

"What on earth? Dodo, you have your own home—"

"Gabel, there are moments when you're so much like your father." Her eyes filled with tears. "I don't like living alone, and I thought I'd try this for a time. If it works out, I'll sell my house later, when I'm sure."

Gabe looked at Pete, who stepped behind his grandmother, peering at his brother over her head. Gabe's voice softened. "You really think you might like living here better?"

"I want to see. When we talked on the phone last week, Miss Smith told me about the recreational center and the van to take residents shopping. She said the people are friendly and nice."

"I didn't know you had been looking around."

"I haven't. Petey suggested this."

"I might have known." Gabe glared at Pete, who smiled.

"I can help Dodo move," Pete said.

"And visit her often," Gabe added grimly.

"Oh, he's promised to come see me several times a week. Your nursery is only ten blocks down the street. He can run by for breakfast. And so can you." She poked Gabe's flat stomach. "It would do you good to put some meat on your bones."

Gabe grinned, looked at Sandy, and shook his head. "Pete, when you come to work, we'll have a little chat."

"Sure. Dodo, let's look at the apartment," Pete said, stepping inside, out of sight.

"Here, darling, hold Pookums while I look around." Dodo thrust the cat into Gabe's arms and went inside.

The cat hissed and tried to wriggle free. As Gabe swore beneath his breath, Sandy reached out to take the cat, which settled happily on her shoulder.

"You have the right touch."

"Will your brother be here all the time now?"

"I'll talk to him. I didn't have any idea she would move out of her home."

"If she's not happy, be glad she'll move. I wish my grandmother would move here. We only have one apartment left, and then it will mean a waiting list. Uh, Mrs. London is an unusual person. She mentioned your father. . . ."

He laughed and pushed a strand of hair off her cheek, his fingers touching her lightly. "They're not alike. My dad, like Grandfather, is a workaholic. And very proper. Dodo drives a sports car and a mini-cycle. So far, we've been able to prevail on her to stay off the busy streets with the mini-cycle. She should stay off the streets with the car. It would really be a relief to know she's riding in a van driven by someone else." A smile hovered on his face, causing slight creases in his cheeks. "So the name London didn't ring a bell—I didn't make much of an impression."

She looked at the cat, stroking his head while he closed his eyes and purred. "You made enough of an impression." Her gaze settled on him. "Be honest. You haven't thought of me either."

"Are you kidding? I hear by the hour how long your hair is, how tiny your waist is, probably twenty inches—"

"Enough said!"

"I could go on and on and on. Now that we're on the subject of us, how about dinner Friday night?"

"Thanks, but I'm sorry," she said, and felt a twinge of regret. "We have a square dance this Friday, and I'm in charge."

"I'm sorry too," he said softly, making her regret deepen. His voice returned to normal. "I'll try to do something about Pete. I never dreamed Dodo would like to live here. She's lived in the same house for over forty-five years."

"This is a nice place. It's not a nursing home. It's a retirement center. Some people don't realize the difference. My grandmother, for one."

"Seems like she would move, since you're here."

"No. She wants me to live with her, and it annoys her that I won't."

"Family," he said, and sighed.

"I'll go back to the office. I'll take Pookums. He seems happy."

"Pete and Pookums. You have a stunning effect on men and cats."

"Not men—one big kid," she said dryly, but her heart skipped faster because of his compliment.

Gabe ran his finger along her jaw, intensifying her awareness of him. "It's men," he drawled in a deep voice that slithered down her spine and diffused into warmth throughout her body. "I used the correct word. I'll walk with you. I'll see Dodo's apartment if she moves in. She'll have everything here reorganized and rolling within two weeks."

"Great! We could use someone with enthusiasm. Sometimes I'm the only one, and it's hard to get everyone fired up." She was aware of his arm brushing her shoulder as they walked.

"They will be soon. How are the ginkgos?"

"Fine. Everything would be fine, if you could get your brother to stay away from me. Is he going to live with her?"

"No. I'll talk to Dodo. She'll cooperate. It won't make her happy to find out he's been hassling you. She'll probably put an end to it. Dodo's pretty sharp."

They paused by her door, and she glanced beyond him.

"Here they come, and Pete is grinning from ear to ear," Sandy said. "He's going to ruin my job."

"No, he won't. I'll take him with me now. Want to go out after the square dance? We can have a drink. If you don't drink we can have a malt."

She laughed and looked into blue eyes. "I'm sorry. I have a date afterwards."

"You weren't going to mention what you had planned after the square dance!"

"Sorry," she said, and meant it. His blue eyes

were fringed by the thickest dark lashes she had
ever seen on a man, softening the planes and
angles of his features.

Before Gabe could speak, Dodo and Pete joined
them. Dodo reached for Pookums. "The apartment
is perfect. I can't wait to move in. Pete said he
would help me. And Pookums likes you! Isn't that
nice? He doesn't like everyone."

"Do you want to sign the papers now?" Sandy
asked.

"Yes. How soon can I move?"

"It's vacant. When we sign the papers, you give
me a check, I'll give you the key, and the apartment
is yours."

"Oh, goody! I just can't wait to meet everyone."

Smiling at Sandy, Gabe held open the door.

They entered the office, concluded the transac-
tion, and everyone left. Sandy stood at the window
a moment, wondering what would have happened
if she had been free to accept Gabe's invitation for
Friday night.

Sandy kicked off her shoes, tossed down the
keys to the van, and stretched. She had just
returned from taking a vanload of Casa Grande
residents to the shopping center and grocery. Outside, a car door slammed. She walked to the
window and glanced out, and her heart skipped as
she saw Gabe London crossing the lawn toward
her door.

She watched his purposeful stride, his brown
boots showing beneath his tight, faded jeans. In
his fists was a wad of papers; his jaw was thrust
forward, and she suspected he had a streak of

stubbornness. A flash of annoyance came as she thought of the Londons. She had a word or two to say to Mr. Gabel London!

She opened the front door and her irritation momentarily went on hold. In the past two weeks she had tried to ignore memories of Gabe London, telling herself he hadn't really looked the way she remembered. He looked exactly the way she remembered . . . and more. Gabe London did have the sexiest eyes she had ever seen. And his sexy eyes lowered, lashes coming down as he slowly looked at her yellow T-shirt, her narrow waist, her faded jeans and bare feet. Her mind cleared, and annoyance surged back like an ocean wave.

"Are you through or would you like a snapshot!"

He looked up and smiled. "Sorry. I was carried away by the view."

Her cheeks became hot while she glared at him, but her anger was diminished by his answer and his smile. He waved slips of paper beneath her nose.

"Pete is out working on yards today. I was going over the books and I discovered he has spent almost his whole month's salary on plants."

"You drove out here to tell me that!" Her irritation increased. "Look at this. I need a machete to get off my porch!" Her gaze swept over the mass of greenery that filled the tiny porch, the swing, and the steps.

"Can't you refuse them?"

"No, I've tried. They come delivered by your truck, and the driver always says he has to leave them. I've tried to give them away to people here, but these are big plants and our apartments are small. And I can't bear to kill a thriving plant. I've given plants to residents. I've given them to friends. I've given them to the church. I've thought about having a plant sale, but your brother would come!"

"Look, I'm not the one who sent them. Don't use that tone with me."

"Don't you use that tone with me, Mr. London! I'm surprised you're still in business. Half of your stock is at my place. Would you like to see the other plants? Just come in." She stepped inside and held the door open.

His boots scraped on the porch, then his steps were silent as he walked along the red-carpeted hallway. At the living-room door, he paused. In a cheerful, cluttered room, blue chintz-covered chairs, bright red pillows, and an oval red rug were partially hidden by baskets, pots, and long planters that held an assortment of greenery. Ivy covered the mantel, schefflera hid the fireplace, philodendron trailed from the tables, and dieffenbachia blocked some of the light from the sunny windows.

While Gabe stood in silence, gazing at the plants, his fingers were splayed on his slender hips. The faint scent of evergreen assailed Sandy as she inhaled deeply.

"You don't have much to say about this!"

"I'm stupefied. I've never seen anything like it before." He shook his head, and the corners of his mouth twitched suspiciously.

"Your brother stays by the hour with Dodo. He walks Pookums. Who ever heard of walking a cat on a leash?"

"Dodo's always walked Pookums. Pookums rides

on the back of the mini-cycle." Gabe rubbed his jaw and pursed his lips.

"If you laugh, so help me, I'll crown you with one of these pots!"

"I'm sorry, but Pete is really off the deep end this time."

"He walks Pookums around and around my house. When I came in with my date last Saturday night—"

"I thought you said the guy in Washington D.C. gets in the way of other men."

"I talk too much," she mumbled. "He does."

"You had a date two weeks ago on Friday night, last Saturday night—you must be getting over the senator." Wide blue eyes were intense, and she looked away.

"How'd you know it was Senator Tarleton?"

"Pete told me. Are you in love with someone you're dating now?"

"For a man who wanted to inquire about plants, you're getting very personal. The guys I go out with are just friends."

"Guys?"

"Friends," she said emphatically, wondering how they got away from the subject of plants. "My Friday-night date left in a huff and hasn't called since. He thinks I'm dating Pete."

Gabe ducked his head and rubbed the toe of his boot against the carpet.

"That's not funny, Mr. London," she snapped, getting angry again.

"Don't get in a snit."

"Then don't you laugh about Jeff's refusing to call again. And Clay almost got in a fight with Pete."

"Clay, Jeff, Pete . . . holy smoke!" He frowned at her.

"They're just friends. I've known Clay since high school and I go to church with Jeff. It doesn't mean a thing. Why am I explaining my dating life to you?"

"It's of keen interest to me."

"It can't be," she said, but she saw a challenge in his eyes that took her breath away.

"Can't you convince Pete you're too deeply in love with one of those guys to go out with him?"

"No! Pete hides in the bushes or walks Pookums and eavesdrops on my good-night conversations. He knows they're just friends. He's driving me crazy."

"I thought Dodo would put a stop to some of this."

"Your grandmother!" Sandy threw up her hands. "Some help she is! I had a talk with her, and your grandmother is as bad as Pete. You know what she said? She patted my knee and said, 'You're just what this family needs.' "

"Dodo said that?" His eyes widened. "She can't want you and Pete to date! He acts like he's fourteen years old, while you—" Abruptly his mouth snapped shut as his brows arched, and he stared at her with obvious curiosity.

For the first time Sandy realized which grandson Dodo had in mind, and she wished she hadn't brought up Dodo and her remarks. She felt her cheeks grow hot and tried to think of some way to change the topic of conversation.

"What else did Dodo say?"

"Not much. That wasn't important. Why don't you take some plants back with you? Resell them!

Give them away to motorists who pass the nursery. The first ten people who drive by in the morning get a free plant." She realized she was chattering, but she wanted him to go. He was as disturbing as a live wire around water.

"Sandy, what did she say?"

"Stop looking at me like that!" She felt as if two bright blue lasers were piercing through her brain. "She said hmmmmmmmm."

"I didn't hear you."

There was no hope of escape. "She said I'm just what your family needs, 'a woman with a heart.' "

"You don't say!" He blinked and leaned closer. The fresh smell of evergreen was stronger. She breathed deeply, losing her anger, her wits, her ability to talk. She said softly, "You always smell so nice."

"I work around plants."

"You smell like aspen and spruce on a clear day. . . ." And he was leaning closer. He looked at her lips and she couldn't breathe at all. What was there about Gabe London that stopped all her inner workings and recharged them on a new current? "Oh!" The word came out softly as she gazed up into his eyes.

His voice became husky. "Sandy, I remember how it felt to hold you in my arms. Nice, so very nice." He reached out, his hand going around her waist. His head dipped down and his lips grazed hers, and it was as wonderful as she had remembered. It was better than she had remembered. She tilted her head back and closed her eyes, sliding her hands on his chest, over muscles and warm flesh.

His mouth possessed hers, his tongue thrust

into her mouth, and something seemed to explode in her loins. Her pulse roared in her ears as she melted into his arms. He crushed her to him, holding her close enough to feel his thudding heart, while his kiss deepened. In that moment Gabe London lost the status of "just friends" forever.

Above the hammering of her heart she heard a steady rapping. Finally she realized the rapping was something besides her pulse rate. Startled, she pulled away, clinging to his strong arms as if she were dizzy. "There's a noise . . ."

The rapping came again, and she turned. Dodo's nose was pressed against the front window. She smiled and waved.

"Dodo! Dammit!" Gabe went to the door.

Dodo climbed onto the mini-cycle, which sputtered off down the street.

As she drove away, Gabe stared after her, then closed the door. "Now, why did she do that?"

Sandy's embarrassment was replaced by amusement. "She's as bad as Pete. I can't believe it, but she must want me to go out with him and doesn't want you to kiss me."

He scowled. "Well, that's not funny!"

"What happened to your sense of humor, which was so pronounced a few minutes ago?"

"I don't like getting interrupted during the hottest kisses ever."

Her pulse jumped again, and an invisible current sizzled between them. She turned around so she wouldn't have to look into deep blue eyes that carried a sensual invitation to walk right back into his arms.

"As I was telling you about Pete before we were sidetracked—"

"My kisses are a sidetrack? And do we have to discuss Pete? I'd rather get back to the way we were," he said softly, and started toward her.

She moved away and tried to keep her voice normal. "Well, I want you to know that it's not only plants he has bombarded me with. Come here." She left, giving Gabe no choice but to follow her into the kitchen, where five boxes of candy were stacked on the table.

"Holy smoke, the kid must spend every penny on you! Two girls called him this week and left messages for him. It isn't as though he hasn't ever dated or had a crush."

She waved her hand at the table. "Well, I wish they would call here. I'd give them some plants and candy. I can't give the candy away because most of the residents can't eat it. Here, you take a box. Dodo said you needed fattening up."

"You think I'm too skinny?" he asked with great innocence.

"Not really."

"You didn't look to see."

She wished she didn't blush easily, but she did, and had to live with it. "I've noticed. Please, do something with your brother. I've tried to reason with him. I've tried anger. I've done everything I can think of, and he is a mule. A balky, block-headed pest of a mule!"

Gabe caught locks of her hair and twirled them in his fingers, looking down at the golden strands. She saw a twitch in his cheek.

"You're laughing."

"Maybe so." He stared at her, his eyes dancing, and she couldn't hold back a smile.

As they both laughed, he placed his hands on her

shoulders. His fingers held her lightly, his hands were still, yet all her attention focused on them. Her flesh tingled, and she was tempted to tilt her lips up again. "I can't think of anything to do to get rid of him."

Gazing at her solemnly, Gabe said, "I can. If you'll go out with me for a while, if he feels I'm seriously interested in you, he'll stop being a nuisance."

"Oh, no!"

"Oh, yes. It's a perfect solution."

The offer hung between them, an invisible challenge dangling in the air with it. Her pulse raced as she gazed into deep blue eyes that silently coaxed her to accept.

"What about the cute redhead?"

"I can explain to her. She's broad-minded. She dates someone else too."

"What about Clay? Do I tell him to get lost?"

"Explain it to him. If he's such a good friend, he'll understand."

"Jeff didn't."

"Maybe it's more than friendship to Jeff." He moved his hands higher. When he touched her throat, she felt her temperature jump. The kitchen became hot, her lips dry. As she tilted her head, golden hair spilled over his hand and wrist.

"You think that's a good idea?"

"Best ever."

She smiled, excitement generating tiny electric currents. "Maybe it'll work. How long do you think it'll take? I should tell Clay and Chip."

"Who's Chip?"

"Another friend."

"You have a lot of friends."

"They're really just friends," she said, her attention on his hands. "I've known them for years. How long do you think this will take?"

"I'd say two or three weeks at least," he said solemnly.

"I'm so desperate, I'll try anything."

"Oh, thanks!"

She touched his chin. "Any old straw in the wind!"

His hands slid down to her waist to pull her to him. "What a task I've taken on. Let's make it four weeks, just to be sure."

"I can tell you're making a giant sacrifice," she said teasingly, her voice breathless as he pulled her even closer. His eyes twinkled with merriment, but the heated look in their depths made her heart pound.

"Whatever I can do to help a damsel in distress." His lips brushed her temple. "And four weeks is really"—his lips trailed to her ear, and she closed her eyes—"a very short time. But we'll have to be convincing to discourage him. . . ." His tongue touched her ear.

Her voice was a whispery rasp. "You don't believe in wasting time, do you?"

"The sooner we convince Pete, the sooner you'll be free of the pest."

She opened her eyes and looked at him squarely. "And the sooner you can return to Joan. Are you sure she's this broad-minded?"

"My life's my own. And she is this broad-minded. I'll show you." Picking up the phone, he punched a number. Sandy's wits returned, and she reached for the disconnect button.

"Hey, don't! I don't want to hear—"

He moved the phone so Sandy couldn't press the button. "Joan Zelinski, please."

"That's personal, and I don't want to hear your conversation."

"I told you, she's broad-minded. I'll let you talk to her."

"No!"

He grinned. "Hi, Joan. Are you busy?"

Sandy left the room, stepping outside to the porch. She couldn't bear to listen to his conversation no matter how broad-minded and friendly Joan Zelinski was.

In a moment the door was pushed open, and a hand closed around her arm and pulled her gently inside.

"Chicken."

"That's personal."

"She didn't mind at all. She gave me to you with her blessings. She has a date with someone else Friday night."

She smiled. "It makes me feel better to know you're not wanted elsewhere."

"Thanks again."

"You know what I mean."

"She thinks I'm as bad a workaholic as my dad, and I suspect she's about ready to wash her hands of me."

"Are you a workaholic?"

He shrugged. "I don't know. I didn't think so, but in all honesty, I guess I'm turning into one with the nursery." He moved away and jammed his hands in his jeans, rocking on his heels as he stared at a plant. "I want the nursery to succeed so damned badly. I started a year ago January. In the winter I don't work long hours, because there's not that much to do. It's seasonal."

He turned around and smiled. "And speaking of work, I've been away a long time now. The bad thing is, I'm keeping late hours right now. 'Course, Pete is, too, so he won't be around when I'm not around."

"That's what you think! He eats breakfast, lunch, and dinner with Do—" She clamped her mouth shut as it dawned on her what would happen. And it did. And the prospect alternately worried and excited her.

"So we'll eat together when we can. The sooner we can become convincing, the better, wouldn't you say?"

She laughed. "I'm not that good a cook!"

"I'll bring something in. We'll take care of brother Pete." His arm slipped around her waist, and he pulled her close. She took a deep breath, relishing his evergreen scent, while her heart skipped faster. Automatically, her hands went up to lie against his chest.

"I think this will be the most fun project I've ever undertaken," he said softly.

"Maybe we're both playing with fire. You're busy, I'm busy. I don't want to come out of the next four weeks with a broken heart."

His blue eyes darkened a fraction. "Sometimes in life you have to face a little risk. I took a risk in opening the nursery. I'm running just as big a risk of a broken heart as you, you know."

"Not really. You're tougher, older, more experienced."

"You make me sound like a pair of old shoes."

She laughed breathlessly, but it was smothered

by his lips. He kissed her, and it was grand. It made the risks worth taking. It made the challenge more exciting. She felt his muscular thighs press against her, his long body lean slightly over hers, molding her to his hardness. She wound her arms around his neck and returned his kiss passionately, until they both broke away at the same time.

He looked as dazed as she felt, while they stared at each other in wonder.

The jangle of the phone broke the spell that spun between them. Without taking her eyes from Gabe, Sandy reached behind her for the receiver, and heard her grandmother's voice.

"Sandy, my dining-room lights aren't working."

"I'm sorry." Gabe had the bluest eyes she had ever seen, and when he was passionate, they darkened, becoming the color of a stormy spring sky.

"Are you sick?"

"What? No! I'm fine." So fine, she thought. She'd just been kissed senseless. "What can I do?"

Gabe touched her cheek, let his fingers linger on her throat. Suddenly, it occurred to her that Gabe London might have an entirely different view of their arrangement than she did.

"Sandy, are you there?"

"Hmmm? Oh, yes, Gran." She tried to concentrate on the conversation, remembering the last few seconds. "Do you want me to call an electrician?"

"Will you? And come stay with me. I can't let an electrician in the house if I'm here alone."

"Mr. Thompkins is reliable. We've called him for years."

"Sandy, please come. I'd be terrified to let him in this big house."

"All right. I'll let you know what time he's coming."

"And on your way will you get a quart of milk and a loaf of bread?"

"I'll get the groceries. Mr. Thompkins may not be able to come today. I'll call you back." She replaced the receiver and tried to think. "You know, we're rushing into something."

"I hope so."

"Will you listen?" She twisted her head so his hand wasn't behind her ear. He returned his fingers to her ear immediately.

"Gabe, I want to have an understanding."

"Yes, ma'am."

She took a deep breath, tried to look somewhere other than into probing blue eyes. She tried to look somewhere besides an inviting mouth. With a sigh, she focused on his white knit shirt and said, "I agreed to date, but I didn't consent to an affair. This is solely to convince Pete that you and I are serious."

"Solely," he said, and she heard the soft laughter in his voice. While his lips grazed her cheek, she closed her eyes.

"I'm a very old-fashioned person."

"Are you, now?" His tongue touched the corner of her mouth and then his lips were over hers, and his kiss was more devastating than before.

"My goodness, you can kiss!" she said breathlessly.

His voice was a velvety caress as he said, "I think the next four weeks will be the most fun I've had in a long, long time."

"I get the same feeling I had once when I was at the top of the Connors Building."

"It has a guard rail and a fence, and it's a safe place to see a marvelous view. Fun and safe."

"Those two seldom go together."

"There are no strings. Four weeks is too short a time to get hurt badly."

"It only takes a few seconds to get run over."

"I won't run over you. I promise. Four weeks is brief," he said quietly.

"I suppose you're right," she answered just as solemnly, but deep in her heart she had a suspicion that life might never be the same again. The moment she had passed beyond the point of no return might have been with Gabe's first kiss.

"Getting cold feet? Would you rather have Pete?"

"Heavens, no! My feet aren't cold. I'm just trying to think of the hazards."

"No hazards, Sandy. Come stand under the ginkgo and wrap your arms around me and give me a farewell kiss," he coaxed in a husky voice that melted into nothing any faint resistance she might have had. He took her hand and they stepped into the yard, to move toward the ginkgo. Sandy felt as if she were in a daze, then realized why Gabe had asked her to look at the ginkgo. Pete's vintage purple fifty-seven car had just stopped in front of Dodo's apartment.

Gabe slipped his arm around Sandy's waist, turning her to face him.

"He's here for lunch."

"Who?"

Sandy frowned. "Your brother. Didn't you see him drive up? Or hear him?"

"No, I didn't hear or see my brother. As a matter of fact, Pete was the last thing on my mind."

"Why are we out here?"

"It's a nice place to be. You said ginkgos are magical." Smiling, Gabe lowered his eyelids as he looked at her in a sensual, lazy way. Then he studied her mouth. Sandy couldn't breathe. Standing in the yard, under the ginkgo, a breeze catching her hair and blowing it away from her face, she felt suffocatingly hot. She ached. Her nerves trembled like the leaves of the ginkgo shaking in the summer wind. Her head felt heavy, and she tilted it backward.

Gabe's lips brushed hers, settled, and the best kiss possible was interrupted by a deep voice shouting, "I knew it! I knew it!"

Sandy jumped back, looked around, and saw Pete running toward them, shaking his fist.

Five

"Hon, my kid brother has a temper," Gabe said with laughter. "I can still whip him, but I'm not angry. I don't want to hit him. And he packs a mean wallop." Gabe started toward his car. "It's too much trouble over nothing. You tell him we're dating."

"Me tell him! Gabe London! You're leaving me with Pete?"

Gabe sprinted to his car and slipped behind the wheel, driving off in a roar as Pete swung his fist through the air behind the car.

As Pete turned around to look at Sandy, she shrugged. "Discuss this with your brother."

"You can't be in love with him."

She started for the porch, and Pete caught up with her, blocking her path.

"You and Gabe have a date tonight?"

"No," she said, moving around him. Again he stepped in front of her quickly.

"Friday night?"

"Maybe. Thank you for the ivy this morning, but will you stop sending plants? I can hardly get in the house."

A sputtering was heard, and Dodo came down the street on the mini-cycle. Pookums rode in a basket in front of her, the wind blowing his fur.

"I have to go," Sandy said, and moved to the left.

"Sandy, go out with me tonight." Pete jumped in front of her again.

"I'm sorry, I'm playing Chinese checkers with Mr. Payton and Mrs. Fenster and Dodo."

"That's no way to spend an evening."

"You spend yours walking Pookums!"

"Just to see you." When he reached for her, she sidestepped, waving at Dodo, who pulled into the drive.

Firmly, Sandy took Pete's arm and led him to his grandmother.

"Hi. Here's Pete to walk Pookums."

"I'll be along in a minute, Dodo."

"Petey, you take Pookums. He's tired of riding. And come help me carry in the groceries."

"All you have is that little sack. Pookums is bigger than the groceries."

"Young man, you won't help me with my groceries?"

"Yes, ma'am."

Glowering as dourly as Pookums, Pete took the sack in his hand and marched off beside Dodo as she drove the mini-cycle slowly to her apartment. She glanced back at Sandy and winked.

Sandy went inside, leaning against the door while she closed her eyes. Four weeks. Too bad there wasn't some way to protect a heart. After four weeks would hers be broken? Remembering Gabe's kisses, her knees grew weak. Maybe it was what she needed to eradicate the last, faint memory of Seth.

There was an unmistakable, irresistible attraction that drew her to Gabe London, that made his every word, his every gesture, important. And she knew, as surely as she knew the color of her hair, that Gabe London felt it too. It was compelling, and the first time she had felt so strongly about a man, including Seth. She had known Seth since childhood, and while he was hard to forget, she had never felt the wild, magnetic current she was experiencing with Gabe.

Giving a shake of her head as if to clear her thoughts, she went to the kitchen to call an electrician, then to get a bowl of cottage cheese for lunch before she drove to her grandmother's. As she sat down to eat, the phone rang.

"Hi," came a fuzzy bass drawl.

"You coward!"

"I don't like violence. Especially when my body is involved."

"I'm not sure you'll be such a help if the next four weeks are like the past thirty minutes."

"Did he give you a hard time?"

"Yes, until I was rescued by your brave grandmother. What a knight you would have been—leaving the damsel to the dragon."

He chuckled, a rumbly sound that played over her nerves like warm winds. "One look from the damsel's big green eyes, and the dragon should have been rendered powerless. How bad a time did you have?"

"Well, maybe not really too terrible," she admitted.

"I figured you could hold your own," he said cheerfully. "You just wanted me to suffer guilt because I ran out on you."

"Maybe so."

"There's something I should have discussed with you."

She stiffened and waited, expecting him to try to wriggle out of their agreement. Instead, he said, "The biggest drawback will be finding time to be together. This is the busy season for the nursery, so I work long hours. I don't eat lunch. I don't eat breakfast, and dinner is usually a bite that I grab at odd hours from some place nearby."

"That's not healthy."

"Neither is going broke. I have to make a go of this. I've put all my savings into it."

"You might not be able to date for the next four weeks. I'm beginning to see why Joan Zelinski's broad-minded."

"One thing I know, my ego is going to be several sizes smaller by the end of that time."

"Bushwa."

"What's that?"

"Baloney."

He laughed. "Back to the problem. If I'm working night and day, when do we have our first date?"

"I love the way you're asking me out."

"It's a problem we have to face."

"I'm a problem!" She grinned and tapped her finger on her forehead. "Okay, I'll come down to the nursery and wait, and when you're through, we'll go out. Unless you're too tired."

"Hon." His voice dropped to the sensual drawl that made her lick her lips and squeeze the phone tightly. "I will never be too tired to go out with you."

"Hmmm."

"What a nice 'hmmm,' " he said in a deeper rumble, which sent a tingle from the receiver, through her arm, into her system. "You come down tonight—"

Her eyes flew open.

"I didn't mean tonight!"

"You have a date with one of those guys?"

"No, tonight I'm playing Chinese checkers with Dodo, Mr. Payton, and Mrs. Fenster."

"You're sweet, Sandy. Tomorrow night, then."

"Fine."

"Gotta run."

She replaced the receiver and felt a shiver of excitement. He had to work late, he was taking her out just to trick his brother, yet she was breathless with anticipation. She shook her head, but all the sensible warnings didn't change her feelings one degree.

The next night Sandy dressed in a pale blue sundress and sandals. She looped her hair on top of her head and applied a light touch of makeup, seeing Gabe's smile, remembering his husky voice, all the time she dressed.

The phone rang, and she snatched it up.

"Hi, Sandy."

How could a voice over the phone be so sexy? Her breath expelled in a throaty "Hi."

He laughed softly. "I can't wait. I'm sorry, but we're swamped. I don't know when I can close. I'll get away as soon as possible."

"Have you had dinner?"

"No, we'll eat when I'm through working, if you can last that long."

When she agreed, he said, "See you." The phone clicked, and she gazed at the receiver. The briefest conversation and her pulse rate was humming along like Dodo's mini-cycle.

On the way to London Garden and Nursery, Sandy bought two hamburgers and two chocolate shakes at a fast-food restaurant. When she stepped out of the car, Gabe was explaining to a customer which type of Bermuda grass seed to use. She waved, and he pointed toward his office.

Sandy stepped around the partition and sat down behind his desk in the only chair available, waiting a few minutes until Gabe appeared. His beige knit shirt had a smudge of dirt on a shoulder, and his jeans were spattered with mud. He had a streak of mud on his cheek and his hands were grimy, but her heart turned somersaults and the office brightened beneath a smile that would have made the roses bloom. She smiled in return. He leaned over the desk and propped his chin on his hand, his face level with hers and only inches away.

"Hi," he drawled in his deep voice. "Are you real or a vision?"

"I'm real. So are the hamburgers and shakes."

"Green eyes, rosy lips—who needs food?"

She smiled, but her heart was still somersaulting. She fought the urge to lean forward. He had the most enticing mouth, the sexiest eyes.

"Sandy," he whispered.

"Gabe!" a voice called from a distance.

Gabe groaned, then came around the desk swiftly, scooped Sandy up, and sat down with her on his lap, wrapping his arms around her.

"Gabe," she said in a warning tone.

"Just doing my duty. It's Pete." He held Sandy close, then relaxed his grip slightly as Pete stepped around the partition.

"Gabe, I saw—"

Sandy pulled away and stood up, blushing as guiltily as if she had been caught in a more embarrassing situation.

"Hi, Sandy," Pete said, looking at her intently. He scowled at Gabe. "I'd like to talk to you, Gabe."

Gabe waved his hand. "Any time."

"Not now, later. What are you doing here, Sandy?"

"We have a date," Gabe answered easily. He stood up and took Sandy's arm, letting her have the chair.

Pete's lips firmed. He crossed to kneel beside Sandy's chair and whisper in her ear, "You're choosing the wrong brother. He's a heartbreaker if and when he gives a woman the time of day. My brother is fickle, demanding, particular, cold, a workaholic—"

"Pete!" Sandy shook her head. "That isn't nice."

"Neither is he. He has weird habits—"

"Will you get out of my office?" Gabe snapped, but Sandy thought she heard laughter in his voice.

"What weird habits?" she whispered.

Gabe's hand closed around Pete's arm, and Pete was propelled away.

"Move that row of japonica bushes toward the front beside the new sugar maples."

"Weird!" Pete called as he disappeared around the partition. Gabe grinned and shrugged.

"What do you do that's weird?"

"How can anything I do be called weird compared to his behavior? I'm just your normal, average guy."

"Oh, sure, you are," she answered, thinking about his kisses.

His brows raised. "I'm abnormal?"

She blushed. "Come eat."

He unfolded a chair and set it beside the desk. "What's not normal about me that makes you blush?"

"Do you like chocolate?"

"I love chocolate. Answer my question."

"Are you begging for compliments?"

"Definitely!"

She laughed and touched his jaw, tingling in a reaction to the faint contact. He leaned close and looked into her eyes.

Her breath stopped, then came irregularly. "Go wash and we'll eat."

"You didn't tell me how I'm different," he whispered, and Sandy lost all awareness of anything in the world except his blue eyes.

"Your kisses," she whispered, and looked at a mouth that was a perfect shape, well defined, slightly full upper lip, fuller lower lip.

He groaned, breaking the spell. "You would tell me that when I can't touch you," he said, waving his grimy hands.

"You wanted to know. And I think your dust has already rubbed off on me."

"Oh, Sandy!" he exclaimed mockingly as he started around the desk.

She smiled and threw up her hands. "Go wash! That wasn't an invitation. By the way, I brought some of your plants back. They're in the car."

"They're yours. You keep them."

"The burgers are getting cold."

"So am I." He held out his arms, and she laughed.

"In June? I know better. It's only eighty-one degrees right now."

They laughed, and Gabe left to wash his hands. He returned, ate with her, and then went back to work.

Sandy got up to look around the nursery. She went outside, where Gabe was moving a large potted honey locust. He knelt down, his faded jeans molding to muscled legs, his shirt pulling tautly across his broad shoulders. Locks of brown hair fell across his forehead as he lifted the heavy pot and carried it toward the front. When he glanced at her, he winked, making her feel warm inside.

Sandy strolled between long rows of tables filled with small blooming annuals, delicate pink verbena, and purple clematis. She carefully avoided Pete, but he was too busy to be a problem. As the dinner hour passed, more customers arrived, until the nursery was filled with people. While Sandy stood in one of the greenhouses, looking at rows of green and pink caladiums, a woman tapped her shoulder.

"Will these grow in the shade?" she asked, holding a pot of hibiscus.

"No, I don't think that will grow too well, but I don't work—"

"I need a low flowering plant for a bed that's shaded almost the entire day."

Sandy looked for an employee, but none were in the greenhouse. "I don't work here, but I know there are several plants that grow in the shade." She remembered seeing some in the next greenhouse and waved her hand. "If you'll come with me, I'll show them to you."

Inside the greenhouse, Sandy pointed to tiny red flowers. "These impatiens will bloom all summer. So will begonias and hydrangeas."

The woman leaned down to look at the impatiens. "These are perfect. You don't work here?"

"No, but I'll help you get these to the cash register. How many do you want?"

"Twelve."

Sandy carried pots, passing Gabe, who held bags of concrete mix. She shrugged as he glanced at the pots in her hands. Someone spoke to him, and he turned away. Sandy placed the impatiens on the counter by the register, where a young woman was ringing up purchases. As Sandy started back to get more, another customer stopped her to ask her questions, and within minutes she was helping her second customer.

When she carried the next purchases to the register, Gabe said, "You're hired. You know as much about these plants as some of my employees."

"I know a little."

He grinned, and for the next two hours Sandy was as busy as the regular employees.

She loaded pots of euonymus into a car for a customer and turned to find Pete blocking her path. He halted, holding a wheelbarrow in front of him.

"I told you my brother's weird and a workaholic. Some date you're having. You're working as hard as any of us."

She laughed. "I don't mind."

"This is better than dinner and a show?"

"I like to feel needed."

"Oh, Sandy, I need you!" Pete dropped the wheelbarrow and caught her in his arms. "Sandy! I can't think. I can't work."

"Young man, I hate to interrupt, but may we have our dogwood and forsythia?"

A couple stood a few feet away, beside a car with

the trunk open. Sandy blushed and stepped out of Pete's arms.

"Sure, sorry, but I'm so in love with her."

The man grinned and the woman peered intently at Sandy, who blushed, leaving quickly.

The last rays of sunlight threw pink stripes across the sky, then twilight gradually faded into night, and Gabe closed up at half past nine. It took another thirty minutes to put things away, to talk to his employees about the day's work, and finally he was alone with Sandy.

"You should be exhausted," she said. "What time did you come in this morning?"

"Seven. I got here early to go over books and orders."

"This is above and beyond the call of duty tonight. I think I should go home."

He reached out to catch her arm. "I need to unwind and relax. Don't go."

"Sure." How could she refuse blue eyes that coaxed, a voice that caressed?

"Let's go to my place, so I can clean up, and then we'll decide what we want to do." He reached up and removed a leaf from her hair. "Thanks for the help tonight."

"It was fun. I like plants. Within reason," she added hastily. "I never have unloaded the ones in my car."

"Take them back home with you. They're yours. We'll take your car home first."

"Okay."

He smiled at her. "You're easy to get along with, woman with a heart."

She blushed. "I wish I hadn't told you what Dodo said."

He laughed, and held the door of her car. She drove home, parked in the carport, and climbed into his black car. Twenty minutes later, she sat alone in Gabe's living room while he showered and changed.

She gazed at the neat apartment that looked as if it were the display room in a furniture store. It was beautiful—and appeared unoccupied. Every pillow was in place, the plants were healthy, the magazines lined up in a row on the large glass coffee table. The shelves of the cherry-wood tables at each end of the brown leather sofa were neat, devoid of any personal touches.

Suddenly he appeared in the door, and she drew a long breath. His hair was damp, his blue chambray shirt open at the throat, and dark slacks fit trimly on his slender hips. She felt her heart thud as she looked at him. And, too late, she realized her gaze had drifted down the full length of him, then back up. When she met his eyes, her heart stopped. A faint smile tugged at the corners of his mouth as he crossed the room and reached down to pull her into his arms to kiss her.

Her pulse hammered, and she locked her arms around his neck, returning his kiss for a moment before leaning away.

"You don't have to kiss me. Pete doesn't know what's going on now."

"I didn't kiss you to impress Pete," he said huskily.

"You know, if you keep up these kisses for four weeks, I might get addicted."

"I already am," he said, leaning closer.

"I hear sirens of warning going off in my mind. Are we getting into deep water here?"

"I think we fell into an ocean the day we met."

Her heart skipped and thumped as she whispered, "You felt it, too—"

"You're sweet, but sometimes you talk too much."

"Who's talking?" she asked in a sultry tone, and tilted her lips up to meet his. His tongue touched hers, and a flame licked along her veins, leaving a trail of heat. His arm tightened, and Sandy pressed against him.

In a few minutes he swung her into his arms and sat down on the sofa to lay her back on the pillows. He leaned over her, tracing her face with his finger.

"Thank goodness for ginkgos. I wouldn't have known you otherwise."

She felt tingles dancing from each touch as she gazed up at him silently, looking at features that made her heart pound. His incredibly long lashes, his straight nose, his slightly prominent cheekbones, all combined to create a face that was rugged, masculine, and appealing. Dangerously appealing. Four weeks, she reminded herself. "What's weird about you?"

"Ask Pete. I'm sure he'll be glad to tell you."

"He said you're cold."

"My kisses are cold?"

"I can't decide," she teased, aware that she was flirting with danger. His blue eyes darkened a shade. His breath fanned over her face as he whispered, "Let's find out. . . ."

This time as his mouth covered hers, his weight came down to press her into the pillows. He kissed her until all thought was gone. She wound her fingers in his hair, feeling the short locks slide between her fingers and spring away.

Gabe's hand slipped behind her neck, his fingers warm on her nape, moving tantalizingly down her back, bared by the sundress, down to her waist. One hand rose to her shoulder, and he raised himself slightly as his fingers trailed back and forth across the straight neckline of the sundress. His index finger eased across the cotton material over her breast in an erotic, fiery trail that made her moan softly. She wriggled away to sit up.

"Maybe we should stop. Things are getting intense for a situation that's merely a ruse."

He gazed at her so solemnly, her heart fluttered like a flag in a high wind. "This is in earnest," he whispered. He cupped her face in his hands. " 'Under the ginkgo my lady lives, a golden tree, a part of me'—"

"Who're you quoting?"

"An old, obscure poet," he said in a raspy, sensual voice. His sleepy, sexy eyes made her heart drum, and she tried to summon enough willpower to move away.

"It's getting late and you have an early morning tomorrow. I think I should go home."

He smiled and stood, pulling her up into his arms. "Do we have a date tomorrow night?"

She nodded. "If you want. You have to work so hard right now, are you sure you want to do this good deed for the next four weeks?"

"What do you think?" he drawled, and relief swamped her.

"Then we have a date tomorrow night."

As they turned into her drive and stopped, she touched Gabe's wrist. "Pete's probably around somewhere. He pops up behind the lilacs or from behind the apartment. He'll listen to you tell me good night before he comes out of hiding. That's how he knew there was nothing but friendship with the others."

"The others. I don't like being lumped with others."

"My dear Mr. London"—her voice became a throaty rasp—"you're definitely not part of the crowd. You stand alone."

"Tell me more!"

"That's enough to inflate your ego. Make this convincing, now."

"I'll give it my best shot," he said, leering at her, and she laughed.

Swiftly his arms went around her as he pulled her to him to kiss her soundly. And she forgot Pete London as a reason for Gabe's passionate kiss.

When he released her, she stared at him breathlessly. "Should I say thank you for a spectacular performance?"

"That kiss wasn't a performance. It came from the heart, if you didn't notice."

Her heart had noticed, and hadn't listened to any messages from the brain. She felt compelled to lean closer to inhale deeply the sweet scent of evergreen, to touch his lips lightly with hers.

"You're sweet, Sandy, sweet as chocolate-marshmallow crunchies. . . ." He held her tightly and kissed her again. When they finally broke apart, Gabe stretched, popping muscles as he flexed his arms. He came around to open the car door, then took her in his arms again.

"Sandy, you're so very special," he said a little more loudly than necessary, and she was aware that now his words were a performance. Performance or not, she could enjoy herself without sticky consequences. She twined her arms around his neck.

"Gabe, what a wonderful time I've had!"

She stood on tiptoe, placed her lips on his, and put heart and soul and tongue into her kiss.

His arms crushed the air from her lungs. The kiss went on and on, until her senses reeled, until she felt as if she had stepped into a raging bonfire. Gabe's hands drifted down her back.

"Look out!" someone shouted. Gabe jumped.

Six

"Ouch!" Gabe yelped, whirling around as barking sounded and a commotion arose. Pookums came flying around the apartment, his tail waving in the wind. A large fuzzy dog was yapping after him, and Pete followed, tossing clods of dirt at the dog. A clod of dirt arched through the air toward Gabe and Sandy. This time Gabe fielded it in his hands.

He swore. "You hit me with a clod on purpose!"

"Save Pookums! You know how Dodo'll feel if the dog gets him."

"Oh, for corn's sake!" Gabe sprinted after the cat and dog, while Sandy watched them disappear around the corner of the house. Pete loped to a halt in front of her.

"Hadn't you better be in on saving Pookums?"

"Gabe can to it alone. Give me a chance. You haven't gone out on one date with me, yet you go with him the first time he crooks his finger."

"Where did the dog come from?"

"Around."

"I'll bet you did that deliberately to get—" She snapped off the words as the commotion grew in intensity. "Here they come. You go help him or I'll never speak to you again."

"One date!"

"Help him!"

They heard shrieks as Dodo appeared with Mr. Payton and Mrs. Fenster, who was carrying a broom.

"Pookums! Oh, my darling Pookums!"

Pookums raced between the people and ran around the corner, with the dog right after him. Mrs. Fenster swung the broom at the dog, missed, and hit Gabe solidly across the middle, stopping him instantly. He doubled over, holding his stomach, while Pete ran after the dog. Mr. Payton picked up the hose and turned furiously. "I'll get them next time around. Chase them around again, sonny."

Sandy ran to Gabe. "Are you hurt badly?"

He coughed and wheezed. "Of course not."

"Oh, my goodness! You're the same young man I hit with the trowel. You poor thing. You must hate me."

"Oh, no! Think nothing of it."

"I'm sorry."

"Come sit down on the porch swing," Sandy urged.

"Pookums! Pookums!" Dodo's voice carried clearly through the night, over the sound of barking. Sandy put her arm around Gabe and walked with him to the swing, where he sat down.

"Mrs. Fenster should be in the marines."

"She didn't mean to hit you."

"I've heard that before."

He coughed again and bent over, rubbing his middle. "Who said little old ladies are helpless?

That woman packs a wallop that would flatten a car."

"She's really nice. She meant to hit the dog."

"She was about two feet too high and ten seconds too late. Why doesn't she get Pete? He's always the cause of the trouble."

"Here they come."

"If she's with them, I'm going inside."

Pookums ran past and headed down the street, with everyone following.

"There they go."

"Will you kiss my injury and make it well?"

Startled, she patted his flat stomach. "That'll have to do."

"Where were we?" Gabe asked softly, reaching for her.

"You've recovered!"

"Sort of." His arm slipped around her waist.

"You can stop now. Pete's running after Pookums."

"Let's practice for next time." He pulled her onto his lap and kissed her, swinging gently as he did so. She clung to his warm shoulders, feeling the cool night air on her arms, inhaling the enticing scent on Gabe's clothing as she returned his kiss.

Finally, he carried her to the door, continued to kiss her for a moment, then set her on her feet. He framed her face in his hands. "I think I'm starting the best four weeks of my life."

"I think so too," she whispered, and meant it.

"You're not thinking of the senator now, are you?"

"That's a funny thing. Seth hasn't gotten in the way since I met you. He's just faded into the past."

"That does make me feel good," Gabe said in his

deep, sexy voice that caused waves of heat to fan over her. "Tomorrow night, same time, same place?" When she nodded, he said, "You don't have to work. Sit in the office and read a book."

"I enjoyed it. Really, I did."

"You were great. You're on the payroll if you like it. I'll keep track of the time. The sexiest, most kissable part-time employee in the whole U.S. work force."

"Sure."

"See you tomorrow night, Sandy."

"Are you going to find out if Pookums is safe?"

"That cat is as able to defend himself as Mrs. Fenster. He's probably enjoying the commotion. He's a real ham, and spoiled rotten."

"You know Pookums that well?"

"I had to keep him in April while Dodo toured Europe."

"It's difficult to imagine you taking care of Pookums."

"If you won't tell Dodo, I kept him at the nursery. He's a good mouser. See you, Sandy."

He walked to the car with a jaunty stride that made her sigh with relief. Mrs. Fenster hadn't injured him badly. Sandy went inside, locked the door, and moved through the house automatically, undressing in the summer moonlight, her thoughts drifting over the evening, over Gabe and his kisses.

A week later she sat on Gabe's sofa after work and marveled at the past week. Each night had become a link forging a chain that bound her heart. Gabe was fun, the attraction was sizzling—

and she was one fourth through the time they had agreed to spend together. Three more weeks—then would he kiss her farewell forever?

It had been a more hectic night than usual at the nursery, and neither of them had eaten dinner. After work they had stopped at Sandy's so she could change from dusty jeans to a sundress. Now, as soon as Gabe was ready, they were going out to eat.

Bare-chested, drops of water on his shoulders, Gabe came through the door. He stood, towel-drying his hair, another, red towel wrapped around his middle. "Would you rather eat here?"

She couldn't get her breath, couldn't answer him. His broad shoulders were the color of burnished teak, muscles hard from work at the nursery. A mat of dark curls made a V, curling on his chest and tapering down into a line that disappeared beneath the red towel. Well-shaped legs with firm muscles stood braced slightly apart. Her mouth became dry, and she licked her lips.

"I have steaks in the fridge, the makings of salad. You could stick the potatoes in now. Or would you rather go out?"

His words seemed to come from a distance, barely discernible over the hammering of her heart. He was the sexiest man she had ever seen, definitely the most appealing. She longed to touch his bare chest, to reach out and feel the flesh that was taut and smooth.

His eyes narrowed; he dropped the towel he was using to dry his hair and crossed the room to her.

Each step closer, her temperature jumped. A foot away Gabe halted; his hand closed around her arm. She came up into his embrace, touching his chest, feeling short, soft hair beneath her hands. Desire flamed in her loins, oozing into her veins with a wild, hot eagerness.

Gabe crushed her to his chest, his mouth covering hers as his fingers wound in her hair. She clung to him tightly, and he lifted her off her feet, holding her so that her feet were inches above the floor.

"I've wanted you," he whispered huskily, his breath fanning on her throat.

She breathed deeply, then dipped her head for another kiss. He let her slide down slowly, and she felt the towel fall on her sandaled feet. The only barrier between them was her sundress and her underthings. She felt his arousal, hard and hot through the thin layers, pressing against her thigh. And she wanted him badly, all the pent-up yearning rising as swiftly as flood tide.

She made her choice silently, realizing it was made long before he had pulled her into his arms. She was attracted to Gabe London to a degree she had never felt before with a man. She had never given her heart lightly, and now it had been taken with so little choice on her part. He was important to her.

Her hand slid down his back, over the smooth musculature, to hipbones that were prominent beneath taut flesh. He drew his breath in sharply and tightened his arms around her.

Part of her would always belong to Gabe London. In a deep, womanly way, she wanted part of Gabe to be hers. Sandy wrapped her arms tightly around him.

"Sandy, you're so very special," he whispered.

She trembled in his arms, showering kisses on

his mouth, his jaw. His fingers were deft touches, little brushes of fire that made her skin burn with longing for more.

His blue eyes held her immobile, breathless, as he deliberately untied the halter top of her sundress, pushing it away to bare her breasts. He inhaled deeply, while her own breathing momentarily stopped. Then he bowed his head and his tongue flicked out to trace a rosy orb.

"Gabe!" she cried, and arched back, her eyes closing.

His fingers trailed beneath the upthrusting fullness of her breast, and Sandy groaned. "Please . . ."

"You're so beautiful, so delicate . . ."

"I'm not delicate. Kiss me," she whispered, wanting him desperately.

He cupped a soft breast in his large, callused hand, his thumb flicking back and forth over the trembling peak, before bending his head down to take it in his mouth. His hair tickled her flesh as her hands moved lightly over his hard muscles, exploring, delighting in each discovery and response she could evoke.

She wanted to give him pleasure, to love him fully. She kissed his shoulder, inhaling the enticing scent of his flesh, reveling in his groan of desire.

"Gabe, I'm not . . . I didn't—"

"Shh, I'll take care," he whispered huskily, his tongue starting fiery tingles in her ear.

The words had been an effort, and she became silent, her lips seeking his, then moving over his jaw, lowering to kiss flesh that was warm and damp from a shower.

Suddenly he peeled away the sundress, her

wispy underthings, and stood back, holding her with his dark hands on her hips.

She could barely keep her eyes open, looking at him with heavy lids, her head tilted back while they gazed at each other for a tantalizing moment. He groaned, and scooped her into his arms to kiss her as he carried her into the bedroom and lowered her to his big bed.

He knelt over her, his fingers tracing patterns across her stomach, moving lower as she writhed beneath his touch. He wove a spell of magic that made her cling to his shoulders and cry out, "Gabe, please!"

He moved between her legs, lowering himself to possess her. She gasped, closing her eyes, pulling him close when he paused. Her hips moved up and he thrust into her softness, bringing a cry from her that was muffled by his mouth.

Her hips moved in an age-old rhythm, primitive, passionate, giving totally to the man she knew she loved. She clung to his strong shoulders while he whispered her name between kisses. Suddenly he gave a hoarse cry, shuddering with release, crushing her to him as their union ran deep, beyond the physical, capturing her heart.

Sandy felt an explosion of rapture. His weight crushed her into the mattress, and both lay entwined, spent and heated from their love-making. Finally, still holding her, he rolled to his side and lay facing her. His fingers lifted damp strands of golden hair away from her cheek. "You can't go back now. You're sure that was what you wanted?"

"Very." She smiled and ran her finger along his jaw as he kissed her forehead. "And you knew what would happen when you came in wearing a red towel."

"No, I didn't." He laughed softly. "I swear. I came to ask about dinner."

"And you didn't know what effect it would have on me to see you like that?"

"No."

"And when we were at my house, if I had come in wearing only a towel, you would have discussed potatoes and salad with me?"

Creases appeared in his cheeks. "No. I wouldn't have discussed anything with you. I would have done exactly what I did just now." His amusement faded. "Sandy, we're good together."

"My, aren't you smug!"

"No, seriously. I mean we're good together at the nursery, as friends, as lovers."

He sounded solemn, and she ran her fingertips over his shoulder, wondering how strongly he felt. He tilted her chin up to look at her. "I thought you and the senator had been lovers."

She shook her head. "I'm old-fashioned, remember?"

"You weren't tonight."

She saw the question in his eyes and said softly, "I think we're good together too."

His arm tightened around her waist as he kissed her.

Her heart beat rapidly and she glowed with pleasure, stroking his back, relishing each touch, the wonder of what she had discovered with him. Suddenly, she raised herself. "I forgot! You haven't eaten today. I'll bet you're starved."

"Oh, I am," he said huskily, and reached up to cup her breast in his hand.

"You don't want to go eat dinner?" It was an effort to talk, and she looked down at his tanned fingers, which were so dark against her pale, golden flesh.

"Shh. I'm doing just what I want."

She settled closer and trailed her fingers over his hip. "So am I. You'll get skinnier if you don't eat."

"There you go, calling me skinny again."

"Bones. The very nicest bones ever."

"And you are a soft woman with a heart, just what this family needs."

Sandy laughed, thinking of Dodo and Pookums. "Hey, your tummy's growling with hunger."

He groaned. "Please, it's stomach. Don't call it 'my tummy.' You make me sound like a kid. And now that you've mentioned it, I may be a little hungry."

"You have steaks and salad here."

"Yep."

She rolled away and stood up, looking around for her clothes, remembering they were in the next room.

"Sandy."

His husky voice set every nerve quivering. He lay on his side in bed, watching her, his blue eyes darkened. Slowly, he unfolded and stood up. Her heart thudded, then beat wildly. Gabe was so handsome, tanned, and fit; a narrow strip of white flesh banded his loins. He was male, aroused, strong.

She didn't know that she moved, but suddenly she was in his arms again, and dinner got postponed for the second time that night.

Monday night of the following week, as they entered the apartment, Gabe turned to take her into his arms, then stopped to look down at his dusty clothes. "I need to shower or I'll get you as dirty as I am." His voice became husky. "And you look beautiful. I like green, because it makes your eyes greener. But your hair has to come down."

Her heart skipped and fluttered, and she smoothed the skirt of her green cotton dress.

"This time, don't appear in a towel or you won't get dinner until after midnight again."

He grinned and ran his hand playfully over her hip. "Who cares about food?"

She wrinkled her nose at him, went to the kitchen, and washed her hands. Humming a tune, she set a pan of water to boil and started to prepare a green salad. As she poured tea into glasses filled with ice, she heard a noise and turned to see Gabe standing in the doorway watching her.

He stood with one hip canted against the jamb, fresh jeans on, bare-chested and barefoot. Dark locks of damp hair waved over his forehead, and his blue eyes smoldered with unmistakable desire.

"How nice it is to watch you," he said huskily. He came toward her, and her heart slammed against her ribs.

"You have the most startling effect on my nerves," she whispered.

A melodic chime rang. Gabe swore softly. "Someone unwanted is at the door."

He started toward it, snatching up a blue cotton shirt as he passed a chair. He pulled on the clean shirt and buttoned it, the tail flapping over his jeans as he opened the door. Sandy followed and stopped in the kitchen doorway.

A man stepped inside, and Sandy knew at once who he was.

Seven

An older, heavier version of Gabe London stood just inside the doorway. Both men had startling blue eyes fringed with thick dark lashes. Gabe's father's hair was the same short brown, but streaked with gray. Both were handsome, Gabe slightly broader in the shoulder, taller, and much slimmer.

"Son. I need to see you. I tried to call all day."

"Sorry I didn't get back to you. I tried once, then we got busy and I forgot. Come in and meet Sandy."

"You have company?" Mr. London's eyes narrowed, and swept over Sandy in a dismissing manner.

"Sandy, I'd like you to meet my father, Chan London. Dad, this is Sandy Smith."

He nodded abruptly. "I'm sorry to interrupt your evening, Gabe, but I have an emergency."

Sandy turned away to pick up her purse. She started toward the door. "I'll see you tomorrow, Gabe. You can—"

His arm circled her waist. "Wait a minute. Dad, Sandy can hear this. We're very close friends."

Suddenly Sandy felt the tension between the two men. And she felt Gabe's fingers clamp tightly on her waist. Chan London's eyes became icy, narrowing; he glanced at her and firmed his lips.

"Gabe—" she began.

"I'd like you to stay. We'll have dinner in a while," he said, looking down at her before he turned to his father. "Come sit down."

"I'll set another place." Sandy hurried toward the kitchen, relieved that Gabe had let her go. She didn't want to stay, yet he had seemed so firm.

The kitchen was too close to the living room to avoid hearing their conversation even though Chan London had lowered his voice. It was rough, a baritone, and not as deep as Gabe's.

"I need you at the office."

"Isn't this old gro—"

"Just a minute. Hear me out. I just had my yearly checkup. My blood pressure is out of sight. Dr. Kinnerman told me to take a month or two away from the office. I have to slow down."

"Dad, I'm sorry."

"I didn't come for sympathy. I want you to come back for a time. Take over and I'll go with your mother on that long trip to Europe she's always wanted."

"Have you thought about retiring?"

The elder London said a rude expletive. "That's as appealing to me as it would be to you. I don't want to retire or slow down or give up. And I'm damn well too young. This is temporary."

"Dad—"

"I don't have much choice, Gabe. He said I had to give it up and try to get my blood pressure down or I might not be able to work at all. But if I step down,

I'll lose my business. We've just received two new accounts."

"Turn things over to Jeanie."

"Your sister's a good accountant, but she's not a manager. I need a manager."

There was a silence, and Sandy held her breath. She gripped a knife and looked down at her knuckles. They were white. She ached for Gabe, because she knew what was coming next.

"Come back for the next three months," Chan said. "Only you can run that business the way I want it handled."

"You know how busy I am with the nursery. I can't leave it!"

Sandy closed her eyes. She hated the pain in Gabe's voice. Why had Gabe insisted she stay? She didn't want to hear their argument. She began to chop onion and green pepper.

"Gabe, you're my only hope." Chan's voice rose a fraction. "I don't want to lose the business. I've worked all these years to build it. All I'm asking is three months of your time."

"I'm in my busy season now."

"Don't give me an answer tonight. I know this is a shock."

"Dad—"

"Don't answer, dammit! The least you can do is think about it. Talk to Dr. Kinnerman if you don't believe me."

"I believe you and I'm sorry."

Sandy hurt for Gabe. The tiredness in his voice was obvious.

"Who's the girl?" Chan asked.

"I introduced you, Sandy Smith."

"Where's she live?"

"At the Casa Grande Senior Citizens' Retirement Center. She manages it."

"Gabe, do this for me. I need you."

"You know you can hire someone. Give Jeanie a chance."

"She can't manage the business or I'd let her have it."

"Have you ever let her try?"

"I know she can't do it. She wouldn't take it, either. She lost the McMahan account in January."

"That could happen to anyone. Will you ask her?"

"If you'll think about this, I'll talk to her about it."

"All right."

"I can't run the risk of going against Kinnerman's advice—and I can't live without my business. I've poured my life into that business. All I'm asking is for three months of your time. I'll make it up to you."

"But a few months means I'd lose my business," Gabe answered quietly.

"You just started. I'll help you start again if you lose it."

Wishing she were miles away, Sandy stirred onions, green peppers, and sliced mushrooms in bubbling golden butter.

"Let me tell your mother you're thinking about managing for me, that we can start planning that trip to Europe."

"That sounds as if I've agreed. I told you I'd think about it, that's all," Gabe said firmly.

"I wanted you to go to dinner with me to discuss it."

"You should've called."

"Will you go tomorrow night?"

"I work until very late. As a matter of fact, I work late every night of the week."

"That's why I need you. You'll work like hell, like I would. I can hire someone who's got the know-how, but they won't have your drive."

"Dad—"

"When can I talk to you again?"

"Give me a couple of days and I'll call you."

"This is the second year you've had the nursery. Are you in the black?"

"Just barely."

"Turn it over to someone and step in for me. When you want to leave, I'll buy you another nursery if yours has failed. If it hasn't, I'll give you a bonus that will enable you to expand."

"You know there's more to it than that. I'm trying to establish a name, a service for my customers that they know they can rely on. You can't buy those things."

"That's why I want you. I'll try to make it up to you." Chan London's voice rose in urgency, his words coming faster. "You've spent, what—eighteen months at the garden business? I've put in thirty-two years at the firm! Help me save years of work."

"If I leave now, you know I won't get back into the garden business," Gabe said bitterly. "And if I do leave, when you come back you'll want me to stay."

"Of course I'll want you to stay, but I can understand if you won't. I'll respect your decision. Just help me out now. Give me a chance to get back on my feet, to get this blood pressure whipped into shape."

"With the bonus and the money you're offering me, you can hire the best damned help possible. You can get a manager who'll do everything you want, including working his tail off for you." Gabe's voice deepened. "You want me back."

"Of course I want you back. I can't get someone as easily as you think."

Gabe's voice rose to its normal level. "It's been a long day, and I haven't had breakfast or lunch or dinner. Will you join us?"

"No. You're working yourself to death over a two-bit operation that takes the brains of a monkey."

"I think that's old ground," Gabe said quietly.

"Sorry. It was uncalled-for. I'm just so damned upset I don't know what I'm saying. Son, give it some serious thought. Please."

"Okay. I'll call you. Something will work out. All this worry won't do you any good. The company won't fold if you take a few months off, and you know it."

Sandy heard their voices grow louder. Mr. London glanced at her as he drew abreast of the kitchen. "It was nice to meet you, Miss Smith."

"Thank you."

"Sorry it had to be under these circumstances, but I have a desperate problem."

Sandy glanced at Gabe, who stood with his hands on his hips, his shoulders braced, his features impassive.

"I'm glad to have met you," she said.

Chan London opened the door and Gabe followed, running his hand to the top of the door, leaning his hip against it as he talked. She turned on the water so she couldn't hear their words.

Hands closed around her waist and Gabe reached past her to turn off the water.

"Sorry."

"It's all right, but you should've let me go, so you could talk freely."

"No. You didn't intimidate or inhibit my dad." Gabe ran his hand through his hair, staring past her a moment as if lost in thought.

"The spaghetti is ready to drain. Why don't you sit down?"

"What a complicated muddle things can become! Dad has that company working so efficiently he could probably take six months off and everything would go smoothly."

"You're sure you don't want to go back?"

"I like the nursery. It's hard work, but I love it. I like being outside, I like plants, I enjoy working with people." He picked up the pan and poured the white pasta into a strainer. "You can't imagine how tired I got, sitting in an office working on books and looking at figures—"

"I don't have to imagine. I didn't like it either."

He dropped the potholders, watching Sandy spoon spaghetti onto the plates, then add thick red sauce. "That's right, you're an accountant too. I should've recommended he hire you."

She smiled as Gabe smiled briefly. He looked so pained, she set the plate down to slip her arms around his waist.

He stroked her hair with one hand while he held her tightly with the other arm.

"I'm sorry you were in the middle."

"We have things like that in my family too."

He pulled away, looking at her with curiosity. "You do? Your stepfather . . . ?"

She shook her head. "It's Gran. She's my mom's mother, and she's accustomed to having the world turn the way she wants it to. When it doesn't— pure trouble happens. Sometimes I'm caught in the middle too. Derek, my stepfather, doesn't get along with her."

Gabe smiled and touched her chin. "Families! Let's forget them for a few minutes. My stomach is going on strike if I don't feed it."

Within minutes the spaghetti, crisp green salad, and slices of buttered bread were on the table. Gabe winked at her, reaching for her hand. "I have to touch you."

Her heart skipped, and all appetite fled as she placed her fingers in his.

"I want to get something for you. I can't get you a plant. I can't give you candy."

She laughed. "I don't need a present."

The doorbell chimed again, and Gabe groaned. "If Dad's back to argue some more, I'll get indigestion. Just a minute, I'll be right back."

He went to the door and Pete stepped inside, Pookums in his arms. Pete's gaze went immediately to Sandy, and he dropped Pookums, who ran behind the sofa.

"Hi. Sorry if I'm interrupting, but Dodo's spending the night with Aunt Willa, and she asked me to keep Pookums. I can't, so I brought him to you. Mmm, dinner smells good."

"All right, you can join us to eat, then you go peddle your papers."

Undaunted by the command, Pete grinned as he came inside and closed the door. He poured a glass of milk, heaped his plate with spaghetti and sauce, and took a bite, closing his eyes.

"My, that's good. Sandy, you can cook—"

"Gabe helped."

"Whoever made it, it's great. Dad was looking for you."

"He wants me to come back and work for a few months, so he can take Mom on a vacation. Dr. Kinnerman said his blood pressure is dangerously high."

"You're kidding. I'm not surprised at his blood pressure, but are you going back?"

"I promised him I'd think about it."

"Oh, boy. He must have offered something big to make you think about it. Say, I sold the 'Bloodgood' Japanese maple after you left."

"Holy smoke!"

"Is that good?" Sandy asked.

"It's a sixty-year-old tree that costs almost three thousand dollars."

"Oh, my, that is good! What an expensive tree."

"I'll have to leave sales to you more often," Gabe said. "That's really great! You get a bonus for the sale."

Pete smiled agreeably, and as dinner progressed, Sandy discovered that he was normal and likable in the presence of his brother. All three cleaned the kitchen quickly, then sat and talked, Sandy beside Gabe on the sofa, Pookums in her lap. Finally, Sandy touched Gabe's arm.

"I should go home."

"I'll take you," Pete said, standing.

Gabe laughed and dropped his arm across Sandy's shoulders. "No way, buster. She's my date. Here"—he reached down to pick up Pookums, who meowed in protest—"take your friend to the nursery. He can chase mice until morning."

"Trade you Pookums for Sandy," Pete said, and grinned at her.

"Out!"

"Okay, okay. Dinner was good. See you tomorrow." He stopped in front of Sandy. "Want to kiss me good night?"

"As the man said, 'Out!' "

Pete put Pookums beneath his arm and left. Gabe locked the door, switched off the lights, and Sandy's heart lurched violently as he turned and held out his arms.

She smiled and walked to him slowly, reaching up to pull the pins from her hair and let it cascade over her shoulders.

When she reached him, she banded her arms around his slim waist as his strong arms enfolded her. Sandy felt for his hip pocket and pushed her hairpins inside the snug cloth.

"What's going on behind my back?" he said, nuzzling her neck.

"My hairpins," she whispered, twisting until her lips met his.

Gabe lifted her in his arms and turned for the bedroom. "I thought he'd never go."

The next night Sandy was busy with Gran, but the following evening she had a date with Gabe. Nursery business was as brisk as usual, and he couldn't close until ten o'clock. Sandy waited in the office, seated on a box. He came in and dropped in the chair to make some notations on a pad, then he closed his eyes and rubbed his forehead. "Sorry, we're late. Thanks for the help." He looked at her. "You don't have to, you know."

"I know." She came around to rub his shoulders.

"Aahh, that feels good."

"How'd it go with your dad today?"

She felt the tenseness return to his shoulders. His voice was flat as he said, "He's begging me to come back."

"Have you talked to your sister about it?"

"No."

"You might get her view of the situation."

He became silent, and she suspected he didn't want to think about it or discuss it. She squeezed his firm shoulders, her fingers working down to knead the flesh between his shoulder blades. As she worked she studied him, aware that she had lost her heart so swiftly. She wondered how strongly he felt about her. He was older, more experienced, and his first love was his business—vaguely, she wondered if it was his only true love.

She looked at his dark hair; his head was tilted forward. She leaned down, her breath fanning lightly over the nape of his neck before she fleetingly brushed his flesh with her lips.

His breath went out in a long sigh and he turned, pulling her onto his lap. "I won't get you any dirtier than you already are."

"I can tell you're overcome by my looks," she murmured against his neck.

His hands slipped beneath her T-shirt, warm against her flesh.

"You're gorgeous, your jeans fit so-o-o nicely, so tight—"

She straightened. "My jeans aren't that tight!"

His fingers moved upward, and his eyelids lowered a fraction as he gazed at her with smoldering hunger. "I just said tight. . . ."

"It was your sexy tone of voice," she said, melting in his arms again, unable to resist his coaxing eyes.

"I hear you have a birthday Saturday."

"How'd you find out?" She sat up straighter to look at him. "Dodo. She was at my place when I received a package from my folks."

"It's a special occasion. I'll take off work, and let's go to dinner."

"I'd love to."

"Gabe—" Pete thrust his head around the corner. "Oops. There's a customer who wants you. I was finishing repotting the petunias when he drove up. I told him we're closed, but he said it's an emergency with some red oaks. Mr. Tattersoll."

"I'll be right there. Wait here, Sandy, please."

Sandy scrambled to her feet, and as soon as Gabe left, Pete entered the office.

"What's he got that I haven't got?"

"Finesse."

"You're sure it's not his dark, wavy hair?"

She sat in Gabe's chair. "That might be part of it."

"I thought so. What else? No doubt his eyelashes."

"Sure, his sexy eyelashes, his sexy voice," she said whimsically, her mind on Gabe.

"I can dye my hair."

"Don't be ridiculous! It's his personality."

"You don't like mine?"

"Do you want an honest answer?"

"Maybe not."

"Don't you have petunias to plant?"

"In a minute. They won't wilt while I talk to you.

You know, I've never had this much difficulty with a woman before."

"How lucky for you."

He perched on the edge of the desk, his bony, freckled knee almost touching the arm of Sandy's chair. "Do you realize that you two aren't really in love? You spend half your time at your grandmother's and he spends three fourths of his time at work."

"We're busy people."

"Yeah. Sandy, what's your favorite food?"

"Ham—you don't need to know."

"Ham what? Ham loaf, baked ham?"

"I don't want to be inundated with meat. Send your food bundles to the Red Cross."

"Aw, come on. I just want to know you better."

"Pete, we will never know each other better."

"We're bound to. If you date Gabe, we'll know each other better. If you're friends with Dodo, we'll know each other better"—he paused, leaning closer to touch her jaw—"and if—"

"None of that!" She spun the chair around, pushing away from the desk.

"Aw, Sandy, you don't know what you do to me!"

"And I don't want to know!" She started out of the office. Pete lunged in front of her, stretching out his arm to block the door.

She smiled sweetly. "Move out of my way."

"Please stay. Gabe asked you to."

"He didn't know the sacrifice he was asking me to make."

Pete leaned backward to peer around the partition. "Here he comes. Sit back down or he'll be mad as a hornet at me."

She let out an exasperated sigh and returned to

the chair. Pete lounged against the door, staring at her.

"I intend to hang around. If nothing else, I might have a chance when you're on the rebound. Gabe will only make you unhappy, you know. He's a workaholic, like Dad. He's weird about a lot of things."

"Name one."

"He doesn't wear matching socks."

"I can tolerate unmatched socks," she said solemnly. "I'm broad-minded."

"He likes ketchup on scrambled eggs."

"I'm very broad-minded."

"He falls asleep at the movies."

"That's weird? So do I."

"He doesn't believe in commitment, much less marriage. Have you heard his views on marriage?"

"That's between Gabe and me," she answered, far more coolly than she felt.

"He swears he'll never marry. And he has so many women in his past, he can't name them or count them. You're one of many, many."

"You don't say!"

"Don't believe me, do you? Ask Dodo. Or ask him about Yvette, Madeline, Carol, Nola—"

"No way. The man's past is his business."

"Hah! You're scared of what you'll find out."

"If all those women liked him, he can't be that weird. Pete, I'm too old for you. I like your brother. You're handsome—"

"Oh, Sandy!"

"—enough to find many lovely girls who would be fun to date. I don't think Gabe was really coming back."

"Sure enough. He's—hey, don't go!"

"Move out of my way."

"Yes, ma'am." He stepped into the doorway.

"Oh, no. You get out of the door."

"Scared of me?"

"No," a deep voice answered, and Gabe appeared. He caught Pete's shirt in his fist and moved him out of the door. "Run along. We're closing."

"My lucky brother. My weird lucky brother."

Gabe took a step toward him, and Pete jumped away, sprinting out of the office. Gabe shook his head.

"Did he bother you?"

"No more than usual," she answered, but some of Pete's statements had been like prickly thorns.

Gabe stretched his muscled arm past her head, bracing his hand on the wall to lean closer to her, his body warmth obliterating doubt and concern. His voice lowered. "Maybe we're not convincing enough."

"Maybe not." She sounded breathless, but she didn't care.

He bent down to kiss her throat, whispering, "Is he looking in the window?"

Inhaling the evergreen scent on his clothes, a faint trace of the smell of damp earth, she turned her head, almost closing her eyes. "As a matter . . . of . . . fact, he is," she murmured. "But you don't have to do this now. . . ."

"Really?" He kissed her cheek, the corner of her mouth; his tongue traced her lips. "Put your arms around me, Sandy, so we'll look convincing."

"Yes, sir . . ."

The kiss destroyed her thought processes. She forgot Pete and her surroundings, until Gabe paused. "Let's get out of here. Let's go home."

"I thought you'd never ask."

He grinned and switched off a light. There was a crash of pots outside, footsteps, and then a car motor sputtered and faded.

Gabe shook his head as he closed up. "Pete never has been this way before." He paused to look at her across the counter, and she felt her nerves heat to a smoldering flame from the blatant approval in his eyes. "Of course, I can understand why."

"Sure. I'll get my purse."

He chuckled, and stepped in front of her. "I love it when you blush."

"Is that why you say those things? And look at me that way?"

"What way?"

"Ha . . . you know exactly what you do with your sexy voice and your blue eyes."

"Mmmm. Let's go before you have to scrape me up off the floor. Talk about sexy eyes and sexy voice . . ."

"We're going."

"I'm sorry Pete's such a pest."

"I'll manage. I think." She stared a moment at Gabe, remembering Pete's remarks about the women in his life. Was she just another in a long succession?

The corner of his mouth quirked in a crooked grin. "Penny for your thoughts."

"Just thinking about what Pete said."

"Oh?"

"He said you're weird—that you wear unmatched socks."

Gabe chuckled. "I'm color blind."

"Can you tell the difference in traffic lights?"

"I know when to go and when to stop."

"Do you, now?" she asked in a sultry voice.

He grinned and pulled her to him for another long kiss that made her temperature rise. "This time we really are getting out of here."

The next night she spent with Gran and didn't talk to Gabe. Thursday night when she arrived at the nursery, a car was parked in the front lot, and she wondered if Gabe still had a customer. As she approached the door, she heard deep voices and stopped.

The door swung open, and Pete came out. Beyond him she glimpsed a man's broad shoulders, and recognized Chan London.

When the door swung shut behind him, Pete stopped, and his frown disappeared. "Sandy!"

"I have a date with Gabe," she said firmly, glaring at him.

"Well, you may and you may not. Unless you enjoy watching a family fight, why don't you let me get you an ice cream cone? I'll bring you back here. Maybe the storm will be over then."

"Thanks, I'll wait out here. It's a nice night."

She sat down on a wrought-iron bench. When Pete sat beside her, she frowned and scooted away.

"I thought you were on your way home."

"He'll do what Dad wants, you know, and then you'll never see him. This is playtime in comparison to the accounting firm. Dad takes on more accounts than he can handle easily."

"You're not winning my friendship."

"I thought you'd like to know. He won't be through this early at the firm."

"Hmmm."

"You have the loveliest—"

"Pete! Do I have to lock myself in my car until Gabe comes out?"

"No. I'll sit quietly."

After a moment she began to relax and enjoy the night. There was a full white moon, a sea of frothy white clouds to the west, stars twinkling brightly overhead. Traffic had thinned sufficiently for her to be able to hear the steady song of crickets. It was a warm summer night, and soon she would be in Gabe's arms. She felt the faintest tug on her hair, glanced around, and caught Pete twiddling with long strands. He dropped them immediately, as she scooted farther away on the bench. "Will you—"

"Here they come."

Chan London came out ahead of Gabe. "Lunch at twelve Monday?"

"Fine. But it'll have to be brief, Dad. And Jeanie should join us."

"I'll ask—" Chan London noticed Sandy and Pete as they stood up. "Evening, Miss Smith. You still here, Pete?"

"Yes, sir, just talking to Sandy."

"Hello, Mr. London."

He nodded and climbed into his car. Pete shuffled his feet. "You two want—"

"Pete . . ."

"Okay, okay. See you tomorrow." Pete slammed the door of his car and drove away.

"Persistence must be his strongest quality," Sandy said as Gabe linked his arms around her waist. He looked at the spreading bank of white clouds in the night sky.

"We're supposed to have a change in the weather Sunday."

"I hope we get some rain."

"As long as we don't get hail." He pulled her close to kiss her. "I thought we'd never be alone."

Saturday morning Sandy marched into the London Nursery and stopped in front of Gabe's desk. He was on the phone. He winked, took an order for poplars, then frowned at her. She tapped her foot in impatience, trying to hold her temper. He replaced the receiver and turned to lean on the counter. "Happy birthday. What's happened?"

Eight

His heart skipped as he smiled at her. He knew something had made her angry, but it didn't change the pleasure he felt at seeing her again. Swiftly his gaze lowered over the trim white shirt that molded to her high, firm breasts, nipping in at her waist, the faded jeans that fit snugly. He felt desire stir in his loins, and he fought the urge to reach across the counter and touch her.

"You told him it's my birthday."

"I presume you're talking about Pete." He studied the golden highlights in her hair, remembering the way it felt falling softly over his bare shoulders.

"Are you listening to me?"

He blinked, and brought his mind back to the moment. "Of course."

"Don't you laugh at me, Gabe London."

He took a deep breath. "What's he done?"

"I'm buried in pink balloons. You can't find my house for pink balloons!"

"Want me to come out and pop them?"

"It is not funny, mister!"

"Okay, okay. I'm sorry you're lost in pink balloons. We'll donate them to a grocery store for a

Saturday give-away. Don't get your dander up over a few balloons."

"A few!"

To keep from laughing, he tried to count the packets of radish seeds on the shelf behind her.

"That isn't all. Do you think I would be down here over a few hundred balloons?"

Startled, he focused on her. "There's more?"

"During the morning exercise program, I had a singing telegram from a muscle-bound Tarzan dressed in a fig leaf!"

Gabe ducked his head, trying to smother his laughter. He chewed the inside of his lip and took another deep breath, facing her again.

"You're laughing."

He couldn't answer. Trying to look solemn, he came around the counter and took her hand to lead her into his office.

"It was damned embarrassing. Most of the folks at the Retirement Center were shocked."

"I suppose so."

"He's nuts! Total fruitcake from far outer space."

"Sandy . . ."

"So help me, don't you laugh."

Gabe could only take another deep breath and compress his lips and remain silent. He toyed with her hair.

She tossed her head, and golden locks slipped out of his grasp. "A band appeared on the front lawn to play and sing 'Happy Birthday' to me. A band complete with horns and fiddles! There is a billboard two blocks from here that reads, 'Sandy is twenty-nine,' in six-foot letters!"

"My present will be a real anticlimax," he said, struggling with all his might to avoid grinning, enjoying the pink in her cheeks, the vivid green of her eyes. He inhaled deeply, relishing her fragrance.

"You're laughing! Dammit, you are laughing at me!"

"Come here."

She jumped back. "I haven't even begun to tell you. Do you know what time it is?"

Gabe glanced at his watch. "It's ten to twelve."

"It is still morning."

"Come sit down and try to avoid hysterics."

Her voice lowered. "I received a call from the police. There are signs—like bumper stickers—all over the stop signs, the lampposts, the street signs from my neighborhood right down the street past your nursery, and they all read, 'Sweet Sandy Smith is twenty-nine'!"

"My, oh, my. The police don't expect you to get them down, do they?"

"No. There's a fine, and I told them who the culprit is."

"You didn't! I guess he deserved it."

"Yes, he deserved it. See, I'm not having hysterics. I'm very calm, considering what I've been through."

"Balloons, Tarzan, signs, a band . . . what a birthday!"

"You're about to split your sides laughing."

He scratched his head, unable to answer or look at her.

"Well, how funny is it going to be when I tell you that all the ginkgos are pink?"

Gabe felt as if he had grabbed a live wire. "What do you mean, the ginkgos are pink?"

"Are you getting deaf? You heard me. He sprayed

them pink and he pinned little pink hearts on the trunks and he hung a seventy-five-foot banner across the front lawn that says, "HAPPY BIRTH-DAY TO SANDY FROM PETE."

"Well, dammit."

"Where's that big sense of humor that was so evident a moment ago?"

"The other things were harmless."

"Hah! How would you like to be kissed by a singing Tarzan wearing a fig leaf?"

"I wouldn't like it at all. Maybe it's washable pink," he said, lost in thought and feeling a slow burn start. "Those damned ginkgos again and my brother. Maybe you should date him."

She narrowed her eyes and stood up to rush out of the office. He caught her quickly.

"Hey," he said, trying to soften his voice as he looked into eyes as unyielding as glittering emeralds. "I was only teasing!"

She stared at him intently.

"Sandy," he said as gently as possible, and pulled her to him. He wrapped his arms around her and held her close, his breath blowing strands of hair as he talked. "I'm sorry I have a nutty brother. You really do something to him, but don't get angry with me because of him. If I couldn't have you, I'd probably act as nutty as Pete to get you."

"You would?"

"Sure." He tilted her chin up. "I'm sorry, but I didn't know a thing about any of it."

"He is driving me—"

"Shh. I'll come out and cut the balloons free—"

"You won't have to. Mr. Payton said he would, and some of the others will help him."

"Did Dodo see all this?"

"Yes. She just smiled and said Pete's going through a stage. You and I will soon discourage him."

"You're too appealing for your own good, my dear."

"Am I really?" she asked innocently, and he laughed, aching to close the nursery and go off alone with her.

"When he comes in, I'll send him out to see about the ginkgos. So help me, if I have to replace them one more time . . ."

"I hope it's washable. Mr. Payton said he would water them down, but if it runs off the trees, will it do anything to the grass?"

"It may be the dye we use when we spray lawns in the winter. If so . . ." He rubbed his forehead, feeling a surge of relief. One glance at her fiery gaze and he wished he had kept quiet.

"Will that hurt the trees?"

"No."

"And will it wash off?"

"No."

"And when will it go?"

"As it grows out and wears off, in time. A few weeks—"

"I don't want pink ginkgos for a few weeks!"

"I'm sorry, but this time I don't have to replace them."

"Oh!"

"Don't get in a huff. I'll come out and look at them this afternoon. You just lock Mrs. Fenster up so she doesn't do me bodily harm."

"And you keep Pete away from me."

Gabe gazed at her solemnly. "I'll try, but he took

the truck early this morning and said he would make deliveries."

"I've stationed Mrs. Fenster on my porch with her trowel. She is to keep your brother away."

"It would serve Pete right, but with his luck, they'll never meet. How about seven tonight?"

"I may run away from home before that time."

He laughed and squeezed her. "You smell so nice, you feel so soft . . . mmmm, lady, what you do to me!"

"You mean, what I'd like to do to you if I had a chance," she whispered, and wound her arms around his neck.

He groaned, feeling an ache spread in his loins. "I can't wait for seven to get here. Don't run away from home—I have a better option."

"Morning, Ga—" Pete's voice came clearly, then faded as Gabe and Sandy turned toward the doorway. Gabe hurried after him, and Sandy followed. Outside the front door, Gabe stood in the sunshine looking around.

"He's gone."

"Doesn't he realize that I would never, under any circumstances, date someone who hid my house beneath several hundred pink balloons? How did he blow them up? It must have taken weeks."

"He probably knows someone who has a tank of helium. I think all his summer earnings are being spent on you."

"Don't tell me things like that."

"Look at the bright side."

"There is one?"

"Sure." Gabe grinned at her and ran his hand along her chin. "You got me because of him."

As she smiled, he felt a warmth the sun could

never cause. She said, "You're right. I'll hold that thought. Gabe, I've been thinking about Gran. If she came out and saw how happy Dodo is, maybe she would consider moving."

"That's possible. I'm sure Dodo would be glad to talk to her about it. Dodo can be pretty charming."

"It runs in the family."

"Thank you. I presume you didn't mean Pete."

"Aren't you funny this morning."

He was aware of customers milling around, that he should get back to business, but he couldn't tell Sandy good-bye. He wanted to look at her, to talk to her, to touch her. He simply couldn't get enough of her. He smoothed the neck of her shirt over her delicate collarbones. She looked fragile, angelic at times, then she could turn around and make his blood heat until fires licked along his veins. He remembered last night, holding her in his arms. . . .

"Are you listening to me?"

"Su—Maybe I was thinking about last night," he admitted, and watched her expression change. As she licked her lips and her eyes darkened, he drew a sharp breath.

"Gabe, I have to go. Will you?"

"Will I what?"

"You didn't hear a word I said."

"You do that to me sometimes. Memories get in the way of conversation."

"Is that right?" She smiled, a dazzling smile that made it twice as tempting to reach for her. He jammed his hands into the pockets of his jeans.

"What were you telling me?"

"I'm glad it happens to you too. I can't keep my mind on—oh!" Her voice sounded dreamy. She blushed and said briskly, "I'd like to have Gran and Dodo for Sunday dinner. Will you join us?"

"Love to," he said, and received another smile that made him arch his brows in curiosity. "I'm that welcome?"

"I'm thrilled you're taking off work. There's one little cloud on the horizon of my happy day. Do you think you could keep Pete occupied here? Gran doesn't have the tiniest sense of humor."

"Sure thing. Anything else you'd like me to do?" he asked with a teasing leer.

"Might be one or two things," she answered in that quick way she had of lowering her voice to flirt with him. "I'll tell you tonight."

"Wow!" He slipped his arm around her waist to walk her to her car. He watched her drive away and returned to work, waiting on two customers. When he had a moment to spare, he began to search the nursery for Pete, and found him at the back, watering ferns.

"You've really done it this time. Don't you know you just make her angry and make her dislike you?"

"Love is strange. I want her to notice me."

"You were noticed. She gave your name to the police."

"I know. I've already talked to them, and I'll scrape the signs off tonight."

"What a way to spend Saturday night! What did you do to the ginkgos?"

"It'll grow out. It's the dye we use to spray lawns. She has the softest hair, and it always smells so good. It smells like roses."

"Gardenias."

Pete lowered the hose. "You like her hair too. Are you really in love with her?"

"Terribly, madly in love."

"Huh! That answer doesn't sound like you. If you really were, you'd tell me to get lost."

"Get lost. You don't stand a chance. Go find yourself a cute girl. Sandy is too old for you, in love with me, aggravated to her soul with you—when did you get so oddball?"

Pete stared into space. "When I saw her big green eyes."

"Hey! Water the ferns, not my feet! Now, look, you're in charge here tomorrow."

"That means you want to keep me away from Sandy tomorrow."

"It doesn't."

"I've never been in charge before."

"Well, you're progressing in your career."

"What hours am I progressing tomorrow?"

"Why don't you work the whole day? I'll take a day off and leave you in charge."

"I smell a rat."

"You don't want a promotion?"

"Does it include money?"

"Ten cents an hour more."

"Good. I need the dough."

"I'll bet you do. What did the balloons cost?"

"Sid did them for me for free. He has a balloon store."

"That figures. Are you through with your birthday surprises for Sandy?"

"Just about."

"What else is on the agenda?"

"That's between Sandy and me. I have a present to give her."

"Want me to take it to her?"

"It would never arrive."

"She won't like it."

"How do you know?"

"Want me to get you a blind date with a doll who is five years older than you and has long golden hair and a sultry voice?"

"Only if her name is Sandy Smith."

"Don't mess up my evening with Sandy."

"If she loves you, it won't matter."

"It matters to me. You just got a promotion. Don't get fired before you earn the first dime."

"Sure enough. Did you ever see such legs? I don't know why she doesn't model instead of working at the retirement center."

"She's sweet. She likes working with the people there. I'm going back to work. You're watering the gravel again. Will you watch what you're doing!"

"Don't tell me you don't think she has the best pair of legs you've ever seen."

"I won't argue with that."

"You know, you're a nice brother, but I don't see what it is that's so all-fired appealing about you. I could give her more time, more attention, more devotion, more—"

"Nervous fits. Water the ferns, not the gravel!" Gabe left to wait on customers and became too busy to worry about Sandy or Pete.

At six o'clock, Gabe rang up purchases, glanced at his watch, and groaned.

"Mr. London?"

A man stood at the other side of the counter, and

beside him was Pete, standing next to a wheelbarrow filled with bags of fertilizer.

"I'm Don Brenner. I'd like to talk to you about a contract on landscaping and ground maintenance for condominium complexes I plan to build soon."

"Step around here into my office and we can talk." Gabe knew exactly where Don Brenner planned to build. For the past two months Gabe had passed one of the sites on his way to work, visualizing what he could do with the land. As he led the way to his office, he thought about his letters to Brenner that had never been answered. He had presumed the contract for the grounds had been given.

Brenner turned to Pete, who said, "I'll ring these up and have the ticket ready."

"Fine. I need to hurry along."

Gabe remembered his date with Sandy, her birthday dinner, but as he motioned to a chair for Brenner, his thoughts jumped back to the present moment.

"Sorry I didn't answer your letters, but I've checked on your work." Don Brenner opened a briefcase and spread plans on Gabe's desk. "I'd like to show you what we're planning on doing."

"Fine. I'm familiar with the development of Woodbriar, because I drive by there often."

"Good. Now, can you see this?" Don Brenner leaned over the plans and began to talk.

By the time they had discussed the landscaping and left the office, Pete was nowhere around, but the ticket for fertilizer and the wheelbarrow with the bags were beside the counter. Gabe took the bags to the car, loaded them, and shook hands with Don Brenner.

"I'm looking forward to working with you." Brenner said. "We've heard high praise for your work."

"Thanks. After I look over the grounds, I'll give you an estimate."

"I'll get in touch the first of the week and we'll drive around the sites."

"Fine. I'll have plans and estimates calculated as soon as possible afterward."

Gabe closed the car door and headed inside, swearing when he glanced at his watch and saw it was half past seven.

"You're late for your date," Pete drawled as he stacked bags of peat moss in the wheelbarrow.

"Yeah."

"I can tell how deeply in love you are."

"Pete—" Gabe clamped his lips together, feeling a flash of anger as he heard Pete laugh. He rushed to the office and grabbed the phone to call Sandy.

Nine

Sandy reached for the phone, then pulled her hand away. There was no point calling Gabe. She knew where he was, what he was doing, why he was late. She frowned at the phone. She shouldn't have expected him to take off early. Gabe was working so hard to establish his business.

She firmed her lips and walked to the window to stare outside at the pink ginkgo trees, the paper birthday banner that rippled in the evening breeze. He hadn't promised anything except to give a convincing show for four weeks.

The phone rang, and she rushed to pick it up, smoothing her trim white cotton dress. A rush of disappointment came when she heard Gran's voice.

"Sandy, I need your help. I'm completely out of milk and bread. Do you mind bringing some over? I'd like to see you too. I have your birthday present."

"Gran, I have a dinner date. I'll call him and then I'll be over. We can go out a little later."

"I was in hopes you could stay."

"I'll stay awhile. I'll see you soon."

"Do you mind going by the grocery?"

"No, of course not." Sandy replaced the receiver, frowning as she dialed the nursery.

"London Garden and Nursery," a masculine voice said.

"Mr. Gabe London, please."

"Sandy!"

"Pete, may I speak to Gabe now?"

"He's out in front with a customer." His voice dropped to a husky level. "Sweetie, can I help you?"

"You've done enough for one day! Mr. Payton took down the balloons."

"Happy, happy birthday. It could be a lot happier if—"

"Will you tell Gabe I'm at my grandmother's?"

"Want to go out with me instead?"

" 'Night, Pete." She replaced the receiver and stared a moment at the phone. Even though she knew she should understand and not expect more, she wished Gabe had called to tell her he had to work.

She smoothed her hair, which was pinned into a bun on top of her head, picked up her purse, and left, going out through the back door. As she crossed the tiny patio, out of the corner of her eye she glimpsed eyes watching her.

Sandy gasped and jumped, whirling to see who was sitting quietly on her chaise longue.

The largest stuffed panda she had ever seen stared at her. It hid the chaise longue, its furry feet sticking out in the air. In its paws was an enormous card that said, "Happy Birthday."

Sandy sank back against the door, feeling relief that was swiftly followed by anger. She opened the card, scanned the verse, and saw Pete's looping scrawl, which read, "Sweet Sandy, when you look at Pandy remember my heart is yours. Happy Birthday—Pete."

She stared at the enormous bear, glanced toward Dodo's apartment. She put down her purse, slipped her arms beneath the bear's. "Pandy, old bear, I think you're going to Dodo's ho—oh!"

She fell forward, blinking in surprise. The bear was as easy to lift as the apartment. She frowned, putting her hands on her hips.

"What are you stuffed with, concrete?" She grasped a paw in both hands and pulled. The bear leaned sideways, then began to topple, turning over the chaise longue with it. Sandy tried to catch it and was almost pulled down with it.

She stood over it, her anger growing. "All right, just lay there!"

"Sandy, are you all right?"

"Oh!" She whirled around to face Mr. Payton and Dodo. "Pete gave me a birthday present," she shouted.

"Pete?" Mr. Payton asked loudly.

"My grandson. What is it? Looks like black-and-white pillows."

"It's a teddy bear. A panda."

"Oh, that's who you were talking to."

"As matter of fact, yes. I can't move it."

"Want us to help?"

Sandy shook her head instantly, frightened they would injure themselves. "No, he can lie right there in the shade until Pete comes by."

"We'll see you tomorrow at noon," Dodo said, and took Mr. Payton's arm. The two turned toward her apartment, and Sandy headed for her car, trying to avoid glancing back at the panda.

At the two-story Victorian-style house, she mounted the broad wooden steps and crossed the porch, unlocking the east door.

"Gran! Where are you?" Sandy stood in the spacious, high-ceilinged living room of the sixty-year-old house. Mahogany Queen Anne furniture filled the room, along with antique cut-glass vases, hand-painted china, Dresden figurines. A ceiling fan slowly turned, circulating the air.

A tall, gray-haired woman holding a present appeared in the doorway from the hall.

"Happy birthday, Sandy."

Sandy set a bag of groceries on a chair and crossed the room. She hugged Gran's thin shoulders before taking the present. "Thank you. Come sit down."

Helen Crane sank carefully into a chair. "How pretty you look. Here, open your present."

Sandy untied a yellow ribbon and removed yellow paper to open a box. Inside was a linen tablecloth.

"Gran, thank you. It's lovely." A phone rang, and Sandy went into the hall to answer it. Gabe's deep voice came over the line, and she gripped the receiver more tightly.

"Sandy?"

"Yes. I guess Pete gave you the message."

"I'm sorry—"

"Don't apologize. It's Saturday, and I know how busy you are."

"I'll tell you when we're together. We are getting together, aren't we?"

She lowered her voice, aching to be with him, all

her earlier disappointment evaporating swiftly. "Gran had a birthday present for me. She wanted me to come over for a while."

"Then can we go out?"

"Are you through work?"

"You bet. As of this minute."

"Why don't you come over and meet Gran? We'll stay a short time and then go."

"I'll be there in about forty minutes."

The phone clicked, and she replaced the receiver. She glanced toward the living room and returned to put away the groceries and fix a dinner for Gran.

Almost an hour later, Sandy heard Gabe's footsteps on the porch. Her heart skipped a beat, and she stood up to greet him. "I hear Gabe. Just a minute."

She stepped into the hallway and saw a dark blur on the other side of the frosted oval glass in the door. The bell chimed as Sandy opened the door.

Her heart jumped at the sight of Gabe in a navy blazer, white shirt, and gray slacks. He looked more handsome than ever, and she wanted to fling her arms around his neck and hold him.

Pete's words rose like mist off the sea: He doesn't believe in commitment, he won't ever marry . . . so many women . . .

Gabe caught her wrists and stepped back to look at her, his appraisal lingering, eyes dropping slowly, until she felt on fire.

"Gabe." The word came out a whisper, and she tried again. "Gabe, come in."

"How beautiful you look."

"Thank you," she answered, and glowed with satisfaction. "So do you."

He grinned. "I'm beautiful?"

"Oh! You look so handsome."

He laughed and squeezed her. "How's your grandmother?"

"Come see for yourself." She held his hand and led him into the living room. "Gran, I'd like you to meet Gabe London. Gabe, this is Mrs. Crane, my grandmother."

They politely acknowledged each other, and Gabe sat in a chair facing Sandy while they talked.

"How did you meet Sandy?"

Gabe grinned, and Sandy remembered when she had opened the door to greet him in her cheerleader outfit. What was there about him that had made her heart skip a beat from the very first moment she faced him?

"My nursery has the contract for landscaping at the center. I was there to see about the ginkgo trees."

"I don't know why Sandy insists on holding that job."

"My grandmother lives there now, and she really enjoys it," Gabe said easily.

"You'll meet her tomorrow, Gran. She's going to have dinner with us." Sandy crossed her legs, saw Gabe watching her, and smoothed her skirt over her knee. He smiled, his attention seeming to return to Helen.

"I couldn't give up my home. I've lived here for over forty years. I have so much room. I wish Sandy would come live with me."

"You'll see how nice it is when you come out tomorrow."

Helen smiled. "It's getting late. You two run along and have your dinner." Sandy kissed Helen good-bye and they left, stepping out into a warm summer evening. Gray clouds raced across the sky, and in the distance, thunder rumbled.

"We could use a rain. Everything's beginning to burn up." Gabe dropped his arm across her shoulders and she moved closer, matching her stride to his as they walked to the car.

Gabe drove to a restaurant that was on the edge of a lake, and they sat at a table overlooking the water. Gabe was quiet as he stared at a pair of white swans swimming nearby.

"Hard day?" she asked, wondering what was bothering him.

He turned, a slight frown on his face. "I can't get business off my mind. I should be able to turn it off, click, click, but I can't. Until I look at you." He reached across the table to take her hand.

"Are you still coming to dinner with us tomorrow?"

"Of course. You have lovely hands, so soft . . ." He reached into his pocket and brought out a small box to place in front of her.

"Happy birthday."

Startled, she looked into deep blue eyes. She tore open the wrapping and opened a box, to find a delicate gold chain bracelet.

"Gabe, it's beautiful!"

Gabe picked it up. "Hold out your hand," he said, and fastened it around her wrist. Dancing flames from the candle highlighted his features, and she longed to touch him. She caught his fingers and kissed his hand lightly. He turned his palm, placing it against her throat, and his blue eyes darkened.

"Let's eat and go home," he said huskily.

Every nerve quivered, and she wanted to be in his arms. She stared at him, gazing into blue depths that seemed to draw and hold her soul. How much she loved Gabe! She realized that it was more than she would have believed possible. And for the first time in her life she needed a deep commitment, some way to bind him to her forever. Life without Gabe was impossible to imagine.

She looked down swiftly, turning the bracelet on her wrist.

"Hey, what is it? You look so solemn."

She stared at the links of gold. "It's lovely. I'll always treasure it."

"Look at me," he said gently.

She raised her head and faced him, praying that her feelings didn't show. She had thought she was in love with Seth, but, she realized, it had never been this deep, this permanent. She wanted her relationship with Gabe to go on forever. She smiled ruefully.

"Why the forlorn little smile, Sandy? Something's bothering you."

"I'm so pleased with your gift," she answered softly, looking down at it again to escape the merciless probing of his blue eyes.

"Why do I get the feeling there's something you're hiding from me?"

"No, I'm just sentimental, and I love the bracelet." She turned it, trying to get a grip on her emotions.

"Well, it is tiny compared to hundreds of pink balloons, pink ginkgos, Tarzan!"

"This is what counts," she said in a shaky voice.

"Hey, you're about to cry!"

She shook her head, fighting for control. To her

relief the waiter came, and she stared at the menu, seeing a blur of words that finally cleared. "You order for me," she said, and closed the menu.

"How about red snapper and rice?"

"Great."

Gabe ordered, and sat quietly until the waiter had gone. He reached across to take her hand again, his large, strong fingers holding her slender ones. "Now, what's going on?"

By that time, she was composed. She smiled at him. "I was overcome by your gift. I love it."

He stared at her a moment, then smiled. "Did Mr. Payton remove the balloons?"

"Yes. I think the folks had fun with them. They used them to decorate the recreation hall and had a party for me this afternoon."

"Good. Pete finally did something worthwhile."

She laughed. "I hope he won't barge in on us tomorrow. As I told you, Gran won't appreciate his shenanigans."

"Don't worry. I gave him a promotion and put him in charge of the nursery."

"What a relief! He'll be busy all day?"

"All day."

"Good. You can relax and forget your responsibilities for a brief time. And I can relax and forget Pete."

The waiter reappeared with crystal plates holding crisp green salad, and while they ate, Gabe told her about Don Brenner. "If I get the contract on his developments, it would keep me in the black all this year. It would get my business off the ground."

"That's wonderful!" She reached across the table to squeeze his arm.

He smiled, and she felt a current of warmth flow

between them. His pleased expression changed as he sat back in his chair.

"I have an appointment with him Monday morning, and then an appointment with Dad at lunch to talk about coming back into the business." He watched the flickering candlelight, lost in his own thoughts, and Sandy realized how tied he was to his business, how deeply he was committed there—was it so deep it would diminish his private life, as Pete had said?

As if she had spoken the words aloud, he looked at her. "I'm sorry, Sandy. I've been poor company for a birthday celebration."

"You've been wonderful company," she said with feeling, and saw his eyes narrow.

His voice dropped. "Let's go home. Are you ready?"

She nodded, feeling her throat tighten with desire for him. She loved him totally. As a waiter paused at the table beside them, Sandy heard him ask the man at the table, "Are you Mr. London?"

She leaned forward. "Gabe, the waiter's looking for you." She motioned to the waiter. "This is Mr. London."

The thin waiter said quietly, "Sir, you have an emergency call. Will you call this number and ask for Jeanie?"

"Thanks." Gabe took the slip of paper, and as the waiter walked away, he pushed back his chair, his brows coming together in a frown.

"It's Dad. I just know there's no other reason for Jeanie to call me."

Ten

Sandy waited, watching his long strides as he crossed the restaurant. One look at his face when he returned and she knew it was bad news. She stood up to meet him.

"It was Dad. Will you come with me to the hospital?"

"Of course."

"It's not too serious. He'll be all right. Come on, and I'll tell you as we go."

He took her arm and she leaned close as they walked together, Gabe speaking softly to her. "He's in the hospital overnight because of nerves. He's to go home and have a long rest. Beginning right now, no work for two months."

He held the door for her, and they stepped into a warm night that didn't prevent cold shivers in both of them. She knew that Gabe was under more pressure than ever to step back into his father's business.

She sat quietly while he drove too fast, his jaw set in a hard line. Sandy ached for him, wishing there were some way to help. And beneath her longing to ease his worry, there was a sense of disaster. He would be too busy to see her now. They would have to give up their charade for Pete's benefit . . . give up their nights . . . their moments of love.

The red brick hospital loomed into view like a giant prehistoric predator with glowing eyes and a yawning mouth. They walked in silence down the corridors, took the elevator, and emerged on the third floor. As they turned the corner of one wing, one of the most beautiful women Sandy had ever seen was standing in the hall, her golden hair gleaming in the light. She turned to look at them, and then was rushing to throw her arms around Gabe's neck.

"Gabe!"

For a stunned second, Sandy watched them as Gabe returned the hug. Long silken hair swirled against his dark blazer as the woman sobbed. Sandy felt as if she had received a slap. She was tempted to turn around and tiptoe away, then reason prevailed, and she realized it must be his sister, Jeanie. She had pictured a dark-haired woman who would resemble Gabe. And she had imagined his accountant sister as coolly efficient, as take-charge as Gabe, not the woman sobbing in his arms, a woman who was as blond as Pete.

"Shh. He'll be all right."

"I'm so glad you're here. He refuses to let them sedate him until he can talk to you."

"I know. We hurried. Jeanie, I'd like you to meet Sandy Smith. Sandy, this is my sister, Jeanie."

They acknowledged the introduction and Sandy nodded toward the door. "Go see your father. I'll be in the waiting room."

"Sandy." Pete emerged from the hospital room and a tall blond woman followed him.

"Mom, I want you to meet Sandy Smith. Sandy, this is my mother."

Mrs. London reached out and squeezed Sandy's hand. "I'm so happy to meet you. I've heard about you."

"Thank you," Sandy answered, blushing because Pete had probably burdened his mother with his idiotic infatuation. "I'm sorry about Mr. London. Gabe, go on. I'll be in the waiting room."

All three Londons went into the hospital room, while Sandy went to the empty waiting room and sat down, staring at the darkened window. How long she waited, she didn't know, but finally Gabe and Jeanie appeared. He looked drained, and her heart ached for him. As she stood up to meet them, he brightened and reached for her, slipping his arm around her waist.

Jeanie held out her hand. "It was nice to meet you, Sandy, and I'm sorry it had to be under these circumstances."

Sandy shook hands and to her surprise, Jeanie hugged her, saying softly, "I've been hearing about you. I want to get to know you better."

Sandy blinked in surprise, wondering what Pete had said to his family. She was sure it hadn't been Gabe, who hardly saw them and didn't seem the type to discuss the women in his life.

"I'll talk to you tomorrow, Gabe. 'Night."

Jeanie returned to her father's room, while Gabe and Sandy went to the elevator.

"How's your dad?"

"He's fine now. As soon as he talked to me he

took the sedative, and he's asleep. If all goes as expected, he'll be released by noon tomorrow."

They rode down in silence, the soft whir of the elevator the only sound. "How're you?" she asked softly.

For the first time since they had reached the hospital, he seemed to really focus on her. "I'm fine," he answered in a voice so flat, she winced.

"You're going back to his business."

"I told him I'd take charge for the next few months."

Sandy closed her eyes. His decision meant the end of their dating. She knew it as surely as she knew her name. Tonight, tomorrow . . . and for Gabe's sake she should quietly vanish out of his complicated life. At the thought of life without him, she felt a physical pain that was like a blow.

"Sandy?"

The elevator doors opened and she emerged into a hushed lobby, the lights subdued because of the late hour.

They walked in silence to the car, and drove just as silently until he said, "I'm sorry, Sandy. It's been a lousy celebration for you."

"Don't be ridiculous. I'm glad it wasn't anything serious with your dad. You spent part of the evening with Gran. I had a wonderful time at dinner."

He smiled wryly, as if only half convinced of what she had said. "Scoot over here, where I can hold you."

"You sound as if you're trying to be polite."

"If you won't come willingly, I'll get out my club and drag you by your lovely hair."

"In that case . . ." She slipped across the seat, pressing against his side, dropping her fingers to his knee. She loved him, and she intended for the next few hours to blank out of her mind all thought of tomorrow.

When he held the car door for her, he reached down to pull her into his arms. Summer lightning zigzagged across the sky, lighting up dark clouds. revealing Gabe's features, his prominent cheekbones, his deep blue eyes. His eyelids drooped sensually as his voice became a husky rasp that played over her nerves like dancing wind. "Sandy, how I need you!"

He crushed her to him, his mouth coming down greedily, with almost savage need, and she clung to him, responding with her heart in her kisses, her love in each caress. She tried to give to him all the love possible, to make him forget all else, to try to make the man she loved find part of himself, part of his heart, chained forever to her.

Thunder boomed, rattling across the heavens. With a groan Gabe released her and turned toward the front porch. "I'll get you inside before the rain comes. I don't know when we can go out again."

"I understand. Don't worry about it tonight." She could feel him withdrawing. She knew his thoughts were already jumping to the problems ahead. Lightning flashed, and he looked overhead. "Here comes the rain."

The first big, cold drop struck her cheek, then another and another. As they dashed for the porch, she remembered Pete's present.

"Gabe, the panda will get wet!"

He laughed. "Our zoo has a panda you're worried about?"

"No. Pete's present." Swiftly she unlocked the

door. "Help me get him inside. It's on the back porch."

"Help you get what inside?"

"He gave me a stuffed panda."

Gabe caught her and moved her out of the way. "Stay right here. I'll get your panda bear."

Disconcerted, she put her hands on her hips. "You'll need my help."

"I'll manage."

She turned on a small lamp and followed him through the apartment, switching on the kitchen light and the light on the back porch. Rain changed from a splattering sound to a hiss as it drummed on the roof and windows.

"Hurry. He'll get wet, and then I really don't know what I'll do with him."

Gabe opened the door and stepped outside.

"Now, where's this pa—holy smoke!"

She followed him, a spray of rain blowing over her. "You see. I tried to move him, and he fell over. For a moment I thought I might be pinned beneath him and we'd have to call the rescue squad."

"That brother of mine. Damn."

"We're getting wet."

"What are you going to do with this monstrosity?"

"I'll find a child who would like it."

"The kid'll have to weigh two hundred pounds to handle it. Okay, upsy-daisy, bear. Hold the door, Sandy."

She pulled back the screen, trying to get out of his way. Gabe started inside, but the bear hit the door and jammed in the opening.

"I'll get inside and pull. Just a minute." Sandy crawled underneath the bear and took one fat, soft arm to pull. Gabe swore and pushed while she pulled, and suddenly the ridiculousness of what they were doing struck her and she started laughing.

"Do I hear laughter?"

"You . . . might."

"I'm getting wet out here and you're laughing!"

"We can't budge this."

"I think it's stuck in the doorway. Pull, Sandy."

She tugged and laughed, while the bear remained immovable.

"Dammit, of all things. We may have to cut him into pieces and slip them inside one at a time."

"Why are we doing this?"

"You're asking me?"

The phone rang, and Sandy left to answer it, hearing Gabe swearing behind her. Dodo's voice came over the phone.

"Sandy, I think someone is trying to break in your back door! I called Security."

"Oh, no! Dodo, it's Gabe."

"What's he doing out there? It's pouring buckets."

"Sandy, will you come here!" Gabe shouted.

"I'm talking to Dodo. Dodo, we're trying to get Pete's birthday present inside."

"Sandy!"

"I have to go. Gabe's shouting for help."

She heard a police whistle and voices. The panda was wedged in the doorway, blocking her exit, but she could clearly hear Mr. McClanahan, the night security guard.

"It's all right, Mr. McClanahan. We're moving my birthday present inside."

"Sandy, stand back. Mr. McClanahan and I will push the bear through the door."

She heard them both lunge against the bear, saw it move a few inches and stop, wedged firmly half inside and half outside.

The phone rang and Sandy answered, to hear Pete. "Happy birthday, darling."

"I could wring your neck! That bear is stuck in my doorway."

"You don't like Pandy?"

"Pete, you have to come get him tomorrow. Tomorrow, not tonight."

"Yes, ma'am. I thought you'd love him. Most girls love stuffed bears."

"If they're sixteen years old, maybe, and the bear is only two or three feet tall!"

"You like little bears?"

"Pete, it's two A.M. Your brother and Mr. McClananan, our security guard, are trying to shove the bear through the doorway. I'll talk to you tomorrow."

"Oh, Sandy, if I had known—"

She replaced the receiver, only to have the phone ring again.

"Sandy? Are you all right? I see men on your back porch."

"I know, Mrs. Fenster. Go back to sleep. Thanks for calling, but I'm fine. I'll explain tomorrow."

"Well, good. 'Night, dear."

"Sandy! What are you doing?" Gabe called.

"I was talking to Mrs. Fenster."

"Lordy, do I have to dodge her?"

"No!"

"Are you laughing again?"

"Of course not!"

"We can't get the bear in or out now."

"You mean I have to keep the door open?"

"No burglar can move him."

"Someone can crawl through beneath him."

"Let me in the front door. I'm soaking wet."

As she left the kitchen, she could hear Gabe thanking Mr. McClanahan. Gabe sprinted to the front porch and shook off drops of water. He was soaked. His white shirt was plastered to his skin and the gray slacks he wore were dark, molding to his strong legs. She held the door and he came inside.

"You're sopping wet. Go get dry, and I'll give you my robe."

"I don't think it'll fit."

"Wrap a towel around you. What'll I do about the panda? I can't go to bed with the back door open."

"I'll sleep on the couch and protect you. Let's discuss it when I'm dry."

The phone rang as Gabe headed toward the bathroom. He asked, "Do you get this many calls every morning at two?"

"No, it's because of the panda."

She talked to Mrs. Whittenton, reassuring her that everything was fine. When she replaced the receiver, she mixed two glasses of iced tea and carried them to the living room, just as Gabe emerged from the bathroom.

Sandy felt her mouth go dry and all the breath leave her lungs. She had spent the whole evening with him, but the sight of him wrapped in a blue towel brought back memories of the first time he had appeared in a towel. His coppery skin glowed with health, his muscles flexing with his movements. He paused, an amused smile on his face. "Tea at two?"

She nodded, and his eyes narrowed. "Something wrong?"

"You know," she said in a low, breathless tone, "what the sight of you in only a towel does to me."

He glanced at the front windows. "How much privacy do we have? I keep expecting Mrs. Fenster to appear with her trowel."

"She's already called, and I told her everything was okay."

"What a relief." Gabe walked to the window and pulled the drapes, then approached Sandy. She felt rooted to the spot, watching him, knowing that at his first touch she would melt.

He set down the tea and wrapped his arms around her. She put her hands against his warm chest, her fingers tangling in the soft mat of curls while she breathed deeply of the fresh scent of his damp skin.

"Thank heavens for Pete's panda," Gabe whispered huskily, and leaned down to kiss her.

Eleven

The next morning he left early, and Sandy got
ready for church and dinner with Dodo, Gran, and
Gabe. Dodo was the first to arrive, her bright pink
suit accented with deep purple flowers, a spray of
purple feathers, and flowers in her hair. Sandy
greeted Gran with a kiss and introduced the two,
sitting down between them while Gran smoothed
the skirt of her gray dress and eyed Dodo's
feathers.

Dodo said, "I'm so glad to meet Sandy's family.
We love her."

"Oh? I didn't realize you knew Sandy that well.
Or that she'd met your family so long ago."

"It hasn't been so long. I just moved here a
month ago. And I love it."

"I can't imagine leaving my home."

"I'd lived in mine over forty-five years, but it's so
lonely. Here there's something to do, people to talk
to. Next Friday night I have a date with Mr.
Payton."

"A date!" Gran blanched.

"Oh, yes. We're playing dominoes with Mrs.
Fenster and Mr. Whitley. This is a lovely place, and

it's so handy. I can drive my mini-cycle to the store. . . ."

Gran frowned, and Sandy wished the subject of the mini-cycle hadn't come up.

"You drive a motorcycle?" Gran said with the same tone of voice she would have used if Dodo had said she kept pet rats. Sandy knew Gran's hatred of motorcycles and tried to change the subject.

"Gabe will be here shortly. Gran met him last night."

"Does he drive a motorcycle too?"

"No, Gran."

"Sandy, there's a fly."

She hurried to get a can of spray and eliminated the offending fly, but she knew more would follow.

"There's another! Where are they coming from?"

"The back door is open. There's a panda stuck in the door, and I can't close it."

"A what?"

Dodo laughed. "My grandson! He has the wildest imagination. . . ."

"It must run in the family," Gran said stiffly.

Dodo went blithely on. "He gave Sandy a huge stuffed panda for her birthday."

"Good heavens! What will you do with it?"

"I'll get rid of it. Gabe said when he gets here, he'll push it out to the porch and haul it away. Unless you want it, Dodo?"

"Oh, heavens, no!"

While she talked, she heard a car, then saw a head of dark hair through the window.

"Here's Gabe." Sandy hurried to the door and stepped outside. "Hi," she said softly.

"Sandy!" Arms wrapped around her and pulled her close.

She stared in shock at a familiar face and unfamiliar brown, wavy hair. Momentarily caught off guard, she didn't resist as Pete crushed her to his chest and leaned down to kiss her. "Morning, love," Pete said, his voice an octave deeper than usual.

She twisted and wriggled away, staring at him. "What happened to your hair?"

"You said it was Gabe's hair that attracted you." His voice started low and slipped upward to its natural level. He reached for her again, and she jumped back another step.

"You dyed your hair?"

"Dyed and permed. I'll shave it off if you want."

"Oh, no!" She studied him intently. "That isn't all. Your eyelashes—"

"They're dyed, with false ones added. You said you liked his sexy eyelashes. I'm working on my voice."

"Oh, please! I thought he put you in charge today."

"I am. I'm checking on our customers who have problems." He batted his eyelashes at her and leered.

"My only problem is—"

"Your pink ginkgos?"

"That's not why you're here, and you know it! Talk about people with problems—"

"You're so cute when you're angry."

"Pete London, will you go?"

"Do I hear Dodo's voice?"

"You might."

"C'mon, Sandy, I'd like to say good morning to my grandmother."

Sandy threw up her hands. "Go right in."

Pete held the door for her and she entered ahead of him. Dodo smiled. "Gab—Petey! My goodness. I like your hair. Gives you a nice, dignified look. The eyelashes—I don't know. This is Mrs. Crane, Sandy's grandmother. This is my grandson Pete."

"How do you do, Mrs. Crane." Stretching out his long, jeaned legs and folding bare brown arms over his chest, Pete settled in a chair. "Are you two having Sunday dinner with Sandy?"

"Yes. I'm trying to convince Helen how nice it is here."

Sandy noticed that Gran looked as if someone were standing on her toes. She said stiffly, "I don't think I could ever live here. Home is home—only one place on earth."

"Come look at my place and you'll see how nice it is."

"Well, maybe after dinner."

"Good. Have you seen your father this morning?"

"Yes, ma'am. I went by the hospital early. He was supposed to go home around noon. Gabe was going to drive him."

"How was he this morning?"

"Until he saw my hair he said he felt better, but he was still groggy. I think he'll be on some kind of medication from now on. Gabe's taking over his business."

Pete watched Sandy as he made the announcement. Trying to keep her features impassive, she stood up. "I'll get dinner ready. Excuse me a minute."

She went to the kitchen and removed a bowl of chicken salad from the refrigerator, then a covered bowl of sliced fresh tomatoes. As she placed the tomatoes on crisp lettuce leaves, Pete appeared in the doorway. Politeness won over natural inclination, and Sandy asked him, "Would you like to stay for dinner with us?"

"I thought you might not ask."

She smiled. "There's your panda."

"Holy hannibal. What's he doing in the doorway?"

"He's stuck," came a deep voice. "More important, what are you doing here?" Gabe came into the room. "What the hell happened to your hair?"

Pete grinned. "Sandy said she was attracted to you because of your wavy brown hair."

Sandy blushed and suddenly wished both Gabe and Pete were far, far away.

Gabe grinned and stared at her. "Is that so?"

"So I got a perm and had my hair dyed."

Gabe tilted his head. "That isn't all. Something else is different. You don't look the same."

"Can you two carry on this conversation somewhere else?" Sandy snapped.

"Yeah, sure," Gabe answered absentmindedly. "What else have you done? Your face looks different."

"It's just me."

"No, something's different. The eyelashes."

"She said she likes your sexy eyes and sexy voice."

"Oh, is that right?" Gabe grinned wickedly, and Sandy turned her back on them, stirring the chicken salad.

"I had my lashes dyed and I have on false eyelashes so I can look like you."

"Well, that was a colossal waste of time. It won't do you any good." Gabe crossed the room to her and slipped his arm around her waist. "She's my girl."

"It's not permanent," Pete said smugly.

Sandy held her breath, waiting to see what Gabe would say. To her consternation, Dodo called, "Petey!"

"Coming, Dodo, just a minute."

"Pete, why aren't you at work?"

"I'm here to see about our customer's ginkgos. Chad is minding the business until I get back."

"No more leaving you in charge. Next time it'll be Chad." He looked at Sandy. "Good morning, Sandy."

" 'Morning," she answered softly, and lifted her lips for a brief kiss.

"Now, little brother. Come here and put your shoulder to this. We're going to push this bear out of here and you'll load him on the truck and do something constructive with him."

"You don't like your present?"

"Of course she doesn't! Who would like a monstrosity like that?"

"I gave Kim a smaller one and she was ecstatic."

"Kim was sixteen. You're dealing with a mature woman now, buster. Put your shoulder up here and push."

"I was invited to stay for dinner."

"You're uninvited if you want a job for the rest of the summer."

The two shoved the bear outside, and Gabe pushed Pete out behind him. "Back to work with you, chum. Take the panda along."

"Dodo wants to see me."

"I'll take care of whatever Dodo wants. You go to work."

Sandy leaned against the counter watching, waiting as Gabe came back to stand facing her. He lowered his voice.

"All done. The bear's gone, the pest is gone. Now, if we can send two little ladies on their way . . ."

She smiled. "No. They're having dinner. Can you stay?"

"Sure. I have all day today. Tomorrow all hell breaks loose."

"Will it be so bad?"

"I don't want to think about it now." He placed his hands on both sides of her, leaning on the kitchen counter, his face only inches away. "So you think I have sexy eyelashes and you like me for my brown, wavy hair . . ."

"I could so cheerfully wring Pete's neck," she whispered, hardly able to talk. Gabe's lips were only inches away.

"Why didn't you tell me all those things?"

"And build your ego to monumental proportions? You have a sexy voice, sexy blue eyes, a sexy body . . . and if this conversation keeps up, I'll melt and ooze away to nothing."

"We'll take it up again tonight, when we're alone," he said in his sexiest rasp, which was a stroke of fur across her raw senses. "One little kiss, Sandy, and then I'll help you get dinner on the table."

"One?"

"One," he said emphatically, tilting her chin up. He looked at her mouth until her tongue flicked out to touch a dry corner.

His tongue touched hers and she closed her eyes, swaying into his waiting arms, wanting to hold him and never let go.

"Oops, excuse me!" Dodo said. As Sandy twisted away, Dodo returned to the living room, her voice carrying clearly as she said, "They're smooching in the kitchen. Isn't that nice?"

"My grandmother may go into shock."

"She doesn't know people smooch?"

"She probably doesn't want to think her granddaughter is doing it right now in the kitchen. It isn't proper."

"Neither is this." He pulled her close again, his hand sliding over her hip.

"Gabe, will you behave? I have to serve dinner."

Amusement curved his mouth, but he washed his hands and reached for the bowl of chicken salad. "I can put this on the tomatoes. You do something else."

"Thanks."

After dinner, they walked the short distance to look at Dodo's apartment, and an hour later, Gabe and Sandy took Helen home.

On the way back, as they passed the lake, Gabe turned to her. "I own a sailboat. I haven't had it out this year. Want to go?"

"Sure. What about our clothes?"

"We'll manage."

They spent the rest of the afternoon on the lake, and Sandy felt a warm glow each time she looked at Gabe. He had peeled off his shirt, rolled up his trousers, and was barefoot. He was more relaxed, more easygoing, than she had ever seen him, and she realized how tense he had been over his work and his father.

They watched the sun set on the lake, the bright orange rays streaking the silvery surface while gulls wheeled overhead. Afterward, they ate a leisurely shrimp dinner at a small restaurant near the lake, then walked down to the water's edge to look at the moon glimmering across the black surface. Finally, they returned to Sandy's apartment. When they stepped through the door, Gabe pulled her into his arms. "What a fun day this has been."

"It's been good for you."

"I hope it was good for you."

"You need to relax every once in a while."

"You sound like my mother."

"Do I, now?" She answered lightly, but she wondered how much alike father and son were, how much priority Gabe would give his work over his personal life.

"I've waited all afternoon and evening. I'm long overdue for a kiss," he drawled in his deepest voice, which sent tremors through her. He batted his eyes at her, and she laughed.

"What are you doing?"

"Trying to seduce you with my sexy voice and my sexy eyelashes."

When she laughed, he gave her a mock frown. "You're supposed to melt, not laugh."

"It's sexy when you don't try so hard."

"So who's trying?"

"Mmmm, that's better." She wound her arms around his neck and pulled his head down to hers.

The phone interrupted them, and when Sandy answered, she heard Helen sob. "Sandy, I've been trying to reach you. Can you come over?"

"What's happened?"

"Sandy, I'm so glad you're home. Can you come? Something terrible has hap . . ." Her words trailed off, replaced by sobs.

"Gran! What's wrong?"

"I fell down the front steps earlier this evening. I've called and called you."

A swift stab of fear made Sandy cold. "Should I call an ambulance?"

"No! I can walk, but it's painful. I refuse to go to a hospital."

Sandy glanced at Gabe, who stood with his hands splayed on his hips, a curious frown on his face. "I'll come get you, and we have a nurse on duty at the infirmary."

"I don't want to leave home."

"I'll be with you."

"It's so late."

"She's on call all night long. Now, don't worry. I'll be right there."

She replaced the receiver. "I'm sor—"

"Come on. I'll take you."

"You don't have to. You have a terribly long day tomor—"

"Shh. I'm taking you. Why stand here and argue about it?"

She smiled at him and stepped beneath his outstretched arm. "My, aren't you dictatorial?"

"Could be, a little. It goes well with sexy eyelashes."

"Will I ever hear the end of that?"

"I hope not.

"What happened to your grandmother?"

"She fell down the front steps early this evening."

"Sorry. If she can get around, maybe it's nothing serious."

An hour later they stood in the infirmary talking to Hetty, the nurse.

"I'm so relieved it's nothing except bruises,"

Sandy said. "Gran, we have a room available. Why don't you sleep here tonight? I can come if you need me; Hetty will be right here on call."

"I don't have my things."

"We can give you a gown," Hetty said.

"I'm tired. I think I will."

Sandy felt a surge of relief. She glanced at Gabe, who patiently stood several feet away, leaning his shoulder against the wall, his hands in his pockets. He winked at her and she smiled in return.

"I'll be over first thing in the morning, Gran." Sandy kissed her good night, and Helen glanced at Gabe.

"Thank you, Mr. London, for driving Sandy and bringing me here."

"I was glad to do it. Hope you feel better tomorrow."

Gabe took Sandy's arm and led her outside. They drove to her apartment, and on her porch she turned to him. "Sorry about the way the evening turned out."

"Shh. I was with you and it was great. I'm glad your grandmother will be all right." He pulled her close. "For the next few days, you won't see much of me."

"I know. I wish you had gone home and not waited. You have to get up in four hours."

"Three. I'm going in early in the morning to get things under control at the nursery before I go down to Dad's office."

For a moment they gazed solemnly at each other, and suddenly she had the feeling she was receiving a silent farewell.

They leaned forward at the same time to kiss,

and Sandy clung to him tightly, the love she felt for him welling up.

He groaned, and released her. "If I don't go right now, I'll . . ." While his words trailed off, she stared at him, her heart pounding wildly.

" 'Night, Sandy." He turned abruptly and hurried back to his car. She unlocked the door with shaking fingers, then turned to wave, watching him drive away until his car was out of sight.

To the depths of her soul, she felt as if she had just told him good-bye.

The next morning she dressed and walked to the infirmary, to find Gran sitting up in bed, talking to Dodo and Mrs. Fenster.

"How are you this morning?"

"Stiff and sore. I'm in no hurry to get up."

"We're trying to talk Helen into coming here to live," Dodo said. "She's agreed to stay a few more nights."

"Is that right?" Sandy smiled, feeling a flare of hope. "I'm so glad. You know, Gran, we have one vacant apartment left."

"I told her to move some of her things and try it, just as I did," Dodo said cheerfully. Her eyes twinkled. "I told her I would give her lessons on how to drive my mini-cycle."

To Sandy's amazement, Gran laughed. "Dodo, I can't imagine you on a motorcycle."

Sandy sat on the edge of the bed and talked to the ladies for the next half hour, then excused herself to go to the recreation room for the morning exercises.

"I'll go with you, Sandy," Dodo said, and they told Gran and Mrs. Fenster good-bye.

As they crossed the grounds, Sandy looked at the

pink ginkgos. "You're good for Gran. I hope with all my heart she'll move here."

"I think she will."

"You do?"

"Yes. She likes the food, she had a good night last night. When she gets to know some people here and sees what it's really like, I think she'll want to live here."

After a few minutes Dodo said, "When you see Gabel, I wish you'd tell him I want him to move some furniture for me."

"I don't think I'll see much of him for a time."

Dodo looked at Sandy sharply and raised her brows. "Trouble?"

Sandy shook her head. "He's stepping back into the accounting firm. Today he has an appointment with a man named Brenner about a big contract for the nursery. He's going to be a busy man."

"For a few days."

"It's supposed to be at least two months' time at the accounting firm."

"There's Jeanie."

Sandy remembered Jeanie throwing herself into Gabe's arms and sobbing uncontrollably, as well as Chan London's firm statements that Jeanie wasn't a manager. Her thoughts veered suddenly as she realized someone was waiting for her.

A man straightened and came forward to meet them. His tousled blond hair had been tangled by the wind, his skin bronzed by the sun. His faded jeans and a cotton shirt indicated he was taking the day off work.

"Chip! What are you doing here?"

"You're not home often these days."

"Chip, this is Mrs. London. Dodo, I'd like you to meet Chip Franklin."

When Dodo held out her hand, Chip shook it. He turned to Sandy. "Have a minute?"

"Sure. Dodo, will you excuse us, please?"

"Certainly. I have to find that naughty cat, anyway. Pookums! Pookie, Pookie."

Dodo wandered off, but not out of hearing distance, and suddenly Sandy wondered if Dodo was deliberately eavesdropping.

"I've missed seeing you."

Sandy felt at a loss. She waved her hand. "I've been busy—"

He caught her hand and turned it over, touching the golden bracelet around her wrist. "I almost expected to see a ring on your finger."

"No."

Brown eyes peered at her intently. "How about bowling Saturday night?"

Bushes rattled nearby, and Dodo's head disappeared behind the lilacs. Sandy shook her head. "Thanks, but I have a busy evening planned here."

"Sandy . . ." Dodo parted some branches of the lilac, a twig with green leaves wedged in her hair. "Go out with your friend. Whatever obligations you have here for Saturday night I'll do for you."

"Thank you, Dodo, but I can't."

"Oh, nonsense. Go have fun."

Chip grinned at her, moving so Dodo couldn't see him as he whispered, "I get the feeling I'm a pawn in a game. Are we both being manipulated by eighty pounds of womanhood?"

Sandy laughed. "We might be."

"Are you going with someone regularly?"

She stared at him, biting back the answer that

no, she no longer was going with someone regularly. She was merely head over heels in love with him.

"Sort of."

"You and I haven't been anything more than friends. Does that qualify me for Saturday night?"

"Thanks, Chip. We are friends and I hope you'll understand, but—"

"But the answer is no." He touched her jaw with his knuckles. "Is it the senator?"

She shook her head, and his eyes narrowed.

His sigh was audible. "As your friend, I'm glad, but somehow I think I always hoped our friendship would develop into something deeper."

"You're sweet."

"Thanks. I wish I were a helluva lot more in your opinion. I'll see you around. Watch the little old lady—she's a schemer."

"You don't know the half of it!"

They heard a motor sputter and Dodo came down the drive on the mini-cycle. She waved at both of them.

"Good grief! She drives a mini-cycle?"

"Give her room when you drive away," Sandy said with a laugh.

"Why was she so all-fired interested in your going out with me Saturday?"

"I don't know."

"Call if you change your mind."

"Sure, Chip, thanks."

She watched him go, her thoughts on Dodo and Gabe while she idly rubbed the delicate chain bracelet from Gabe.

As the days went by, the conviction grew stronger that Gabe had forgotten her. He called at odd hours, sometimes late at night, and told her how busy he was, how sorry he was he couldn't see her, but the calls became shorter and less frequent.

The second week after he had taken over his father's business, Sandy stood in her bedroom, brushing her hair to pin it in a knot on top of her head. A car passed, and she glanced out to see Pete drive by on his way to Dodo's.

He had been less of a problem during the last week, and she felt her wariness flare into life again. As she watched him park, he turned to look in her direction.

Sandy stepped back from the window, sure that the white curtains would hide her from his view. For an instant she wondered if he was coming to her place, but he went around and opened the passenger side of his car.

To Sandy's amazement, he reached down, and a girl emerged. They ran to Dodo's porch, Pete standing behind the girl as they knocked. He looked over his shoulder at Sandy's, and then they both disappeared into Dodo's apartment.

Sandy stared at the empty porch dumbfounded. Like a shore buffeted by waves, the first surge of emotion was relief, making her give a whoop of laughter. Pete had a girlfriend!

He had a girlfriend and he was hiding her, afraid he would hurt Sandy's feelings! She turned for the phone to tell Gabe, and the next surge of emotion washed over her as curiosity struck her. Why hadn't Gabe told her? The last time they had talked was night before last, and he hadn't mentioned Pete.

Common sense told her that Gabe was so busy,

he might not know a thing about the new development in Pete's life. And then another emotion poured over her like icy sea water. There was no need for Gabe to take her out now at all.

No need except that she was wildly in love with him. It was over. Finally and completely. As the phone rang, she jumped, then ran to answer it, snatching up the receiver while her heart went on hold.

"Sandy, Chip here."

Disappointment was an iron weight. "Hi."

"Uh-oh. I called at a bad time."

"No, not really." It wasn't as bad as the nights when she ached for Gabe's arms.

"I thought I'd try again. Let's go to a show Saturday night. *Green Sunset* is supposed to be hilarious. Would you like a laugh?"

"Thanks, but—"

"You have a date?"

"We're having a square dance here, and I usually go."

"They don't need a chaperone, and you might feel better after a laugh or two."

She sighed. "All right, Chip, but I don't think I'll be very good company."

"I'll worry about that. See you about seven."

"Sure, thanks."

She replaced the receiver and stared at it, feeling the hurt grow. She blinked back hot tears and told herself she had been foolish to expect Gabe to feel the same way she had. The ringing of the phone made her jump again, and she realized how bad her nerves were.

"Sandy?"

"Derek! Are you and Mom in town?"

"No. I'm in Dallas. Claire talked to Helen last night. You really worked the miracle of miracles to get her to take the apartment at the Center."

"I'm so glad, but it wasn't me. The people out here have been good to her and welcomed her. She's making friends, and it's the most wonderful relief."

"I know. Claire's happy about it too. I've got a deal for you."

"Oh?"

"I've got a chance to buy a place in Kansas City that would be excellent for another retirement center. I need to get up there and work on it. Could you move to Dallas and take this one over?"

Her first reaction was to refuse instantly. She didn't want to leave Oklahoma, and she knew why. "Gran's here. I have friends here."

"I know, but you'll make friends wherever you go. I'll give you a hefty raise and pay your moving expenses."

"Derek, that's nice, but—"

"Look, Sandy. Here's the problem. I've tried to hire someone to step in here and haven't found anyone I'd trust to leave it with. The only good application was a woman who wants to work in Oklahoma. She can't leave parents who are in a nursing home there in the city. So if you'd take this place, I'd could put her at Casa Grande."

"There must be someone in the whole state of Texas."

"I haven't found anyone. The other place in Dallas is going great now, but I haven't found someone for here."

"How many weeks have you tried?"

"Well, to be honest, only two. Three hundred dollars more a month, Sandy."

"Three hundred?"

"Plus a car. Plus moving expenses. I really need someone good."

"I'll have to give it some thought."

"Are you going with anyone in particular?"

The question hung in the air like gray fog, obscuring everything else. She gripped the phone tightly. "Not really."

She heard the relief in his voice. "Then there shouldn't be anything to hold you."

"I have to think about it."

"You do that. I'll call early next week. I'd really like to have you here by the first of August."

"I'll think about it."

"That's my girl. Here's your mother."

Sandy talked for thirty minutes to her mother and finally said good-bye, staring at the phone. This time she didn't stop the tears, but sat quietly, without making a sound.

Thursday, she decided she would go to Dallas. It might be easier to forget Gabe if she didn't drive past London Garden and Nursery several times a week.

Thursday morning, Independence Day, her phone rang, and she picked it up expecting it to be Gran, who called with regularity.

"Sandy." Gabe's deep voice strummed over her senses, leaving her quivering in its wake.

"Good morning."

"It is a good morning. I'm beginning to see the light at the end of the tunnel."

"I'm glad!"

"That's the understatement of the year. I hope I

can change glad to something better. How's your work going?"

"Fine." She was tempted to tell him she was going to accept Derek's offer and move to Dallas, but she couldn't bear a good-bye. She hadn't broken the news to Gran, hadn't told anyone, but she had decided to go.

"You don't sound too enthused. Guess what?"

"I couldn't possibly."

"Hey, is something wrong?"

"No. Everything's fine. I'm moving to Dallas soon," she blurted, wanting to bite her tongue.

"You're *what?*" The ice in his voice came through the phone with the chill of an arctic blast.

"Derek is giving me a raise and a car if I'll move to Dallas and take over a retirement center there." Why, oh, why had she told him? It would only make things worse.

"I've arranged to have Saturday night off," he said in a deadly quiet voice. "I want to take you to dinner."

She closed her eyes and momentarily was tempted to accept, to call Chip and explain. Her date with Chip meant nothing, but why prolong pain? "I have a date."

"You have a *what?*"

"Do we have a poor connection? I have a date with a friend."

"Do you have a date with a friend tomorrow night?"

"No."

"Now you do. I have an appointment in twenty minutes. There's no holiday at the nursery. I'm booked solid this afternoon, but I want to see you tonight. Can you go out after work?"

"I'm sorry. I promised Dodo and Gran I would take them to the Theater Center for the opening of the new musical."

"Sandy, what about us?"

"What about us, Gabe? Your obligatory four weeks are up. I think Pete has a new interest."

"*Obligatory four weeks!* You think—" She heard voices in the background, and then Gabe's voice dimmed as he turned from the phone to talk to someone. She heard him swear just before he returned to the phone.

"Dammit, I've got to go. Are you going to be home this afternoon?"

"No, I drive the van for an excursion to the Cowboy Hall of Fame."

"Sweet, busy lady, when can I have a minute of your time?"

Her heart skipped and fluttered, and she wanted to tell him to come right now, that he could have all the time in the world, but wisdom prevailed, and she said, "I'll see you tomorrow night for dinner."

"Huh. There's no time this evening?"

"I'm sorry. The tickets are bought, and I don't want to disappoint them."

"No, I'm sure you don't." Again she heard someone talking to him; his reply was muffled.

"Dammit, Sandy, I have to go now."

"That's all right." She clutched the phone tightly, closing her eyes as she listened to his voice and tried to imagine him, to imagine his marvelous blue eyes, his long, hard body.

"See you soon, and we'll talk."

" 'Bye, Gabe."

She stood staring at the phone for long minutes after she had replaced the receiver. They had a date for Friday night. Her heart thudded with joy, while her mind tried to whisper words of wisdom, that it would just mean more hurt, that Gabe was a busy man. . . . She smiled. She would worry about hurts and parting later. Right now, she wanted to think about Friday night.

She showered and changed into faded jeans and a knit shirt, hurrying because it was almost time to go to the recreational center to get ready for the Fourth of July picnic at noon.

As she braided her hair, she heard a truck and saw the London Garden and Nursery truck stop in front. Her heart skipped, and she stepped closer to the window, hoping it was Gabe.

Twelve

Her skittering pulse slowed as an unfamiliar-looking man stepped down and walked to the back of the truck to lift out two large pots, one containing a lush green fern, the other a tall red hibiscus.

"Oh, no!" Sandy said aloud. She had been wrong. Pete didn't have a new girlfriend. As she watched the deliveryman come up the front walk, there was a knock on the back door.

Sandy rushed to open the kitchen door. Standing on the doorstep, with Pookums under her arm, was Dodo, her hair piled on top of her head, a green-feather headband around her forehead, and wearing jeans and a bright green shirt. " 'Morning, Sandy. Thought I'd walk over to the recreation room with you."

"Come in," Sandy said as the doorbell chimed. "I have to go to the front door. I'm getting more plants. You wouldn't like a red hibiscus, would you?"

"No, thank you, dear. I have all the plants from the nursery I need."

"So do I." She opened the door to face a red-haired man.

"Miss Smith?"

"That's right."

"These are for you. They're heavy. Where would you like them?"

"Back at the nursery. I don't need another plant."

"Sorry, I was told I had to deliver them to you. They're kind of heavy—"

"I'm sorry! Just set them down on the porch." She watched him lower them carefully, noticing a white envelope with a card fluttering on each plant as he settled them.

"I'll get the others and be right back."

"Others? Oh, no! Not again." She turned to look at Dodo, who stood frowning at the plants. "I don't understand why he's sending these." Dodo shrugged.

"Aren't the blooms lovely?" said Dodo. "Do you mind if I put one in my hair?"

"Help yourself. You can pick them all and put them in your hair. Your grandson will be the end of me. Look at that. Here comes the man with two more giant plants."

"They're healthy plants, so green."

Sandy unpinned a card and opened it to find a note in a scrawling hand that read, "All my love, Gabe."

"Gabe!" she whispered, and stared at the card.

"Are you all right, Sandy?"

Dimly she heard Dodo, and it took seconds for her to realize she had been asked a question.

"Where'll I put these?"

She looked up at two more pots of greenery that

almost hid the deliveryman. She was in shock, staring at him stupidly. The plants were from Gabe.

"These are getting heavy."

"Put them anywhere." She couldn't stop grinning at him.

"Okay. Two more and I'm through."

"Two more," Sandy said weakly, suddenly wanting to grab every note and read it.

"Sandy, are you all right? You look pale. You know, I thought Pete had a new interest in his life. He made me promise not to tell you. . . ."

"These aren't from Pete." Sandy unpinned another note and with shaking fingers yanked open the envelope to read, "Love from Gabe."

"Good heavens! You have someone else showering you with plants from the— Who're they from?"

"Gabe."

"Oh, my!" Dodo said it with such satisfaction, it finally registered on Sandy. She looked at Dodo, who smiled smugly. "You'd better find a place for the next ones—the porch will be covered."

"Come inside. Set them down in here, please." Sandy directed the man to the hearth and stared at the plants dreamily.

"Sign right here, please."

She stared at the ticket he held out, wrote her initials, and thanked him, hurrying to read the next card. Each one said, "To Sandy with love from Gabe."

"Dodo, you go ahead. I'll be there in a minute. I have to make a phone call first."

"We'll see you," Dodo said, smiling and holding Pookums tightly. "You're sweet, Sandy."

Dodo left, and Sandy sat down to call the nursery. Gabe was out, and they didn't know where to reach him, but she left word she had called.

Next, she placed a long-distance call to Dallas to tell her stepfather that she couldn't accept his offer. With a grin she couldn't erase, Sandy jogged across the lawn to the recreation center for the picnic.

When she returned to her apartment, she found two boxes on the porch. She carried them inside and opened one, to pull out a small stuffed bear with a card hanging around his neck that read, "I love you. Gabe."

She shook the bear, frowning at it. "Then why didn't you tell me!"

Green glass eyes stared at her, and she kissed a soft black nose, setting him aside while she opened the next box. She dug through packing until she found a smaller box wrapped in white paper, tied with a blue ribbon. She tore it open and lifted out a crystal ginkgo tree, the glittering leaves catching the light. The card lay in the box, and she read, "To my lady of the ginkgos—I love you—Gabe."

He was still away from the nursery when she tried to call. She slipped on a pale blue sleeveless cotton dress and high-heeled white pumps and pinned her hair on top of her head to go to the musical. One last call to Gabe before she left didn't catch him at the nursery, and she gave up for the night.

Through the evening as she sat beside Gran and listened to the familiar lyrics, her mind was on blue eyes, wavy brown hair, and a deep voice.

They stopped for an ice cream cone, and it was almost midnight when Sandy had deposited the ladies at their apartments. She drove into her carport and parked, climbing out to cross her patio. She stopped dead when she saw a man sprawled on her chaise longue.

A scream started in her throat, and she clamped her hand over her mouth. Before she'd made a sound, she realized who it was.

Her heart thudded violently, first from fright, then excitement, as she tiptoed closer. "Gabe?"

He lay with his head tilted to one side, long lashes fringing his cheeks, his chest rising and falling with deep, regular breathing.

He wore blue slacks and a white shirt that was open at the throat. She stared at him, feeling a warm glow like a tiny fire on a cold winter's night. She didn't want to wake him yet. She just wanted to stand and stare at him, relishing the fact that he was here waiting for her.

She moved closer, kneeling beside him. The fresh scent of woods in summer assailed her, and she inhaled deeply. Her heart was brimming with love, and she trembled. The need to touch him, to hold him and to feel his strong arms around her, was overpowering. She laid her cheek gently against the back of his hand.

An arm slipped around her waist and pulled her onto his lap. She yelped in surprise, then settled to throw her arms around his neck and gaze at him in satisfaction.

"Hi, stranger," he said in that deep raspy voice that made her tremble.

"Stranger is right. How long have you been waiting?"

"Too damned long," he said, gazing at her mouth. She felt her lips throb with desire, and it was difficult to talk.

"I meant out here. How long have you been sitting out here?"

"Thirty-six hours."

"You haven't! I just left at seven o'clock."

"Okay, I've been here"—he paused and sniffed—
"maybe two hours." He inhaled deeply.

"What are you doing?"

"Enjoying the smell of gardenias. You always
smell delectable."

"I think delectable is how things taste."

"You're delectable."

"I got your presents. Thank you."

"I heard you tried to send them back."

"That was when I thought they were from Pete."

"That's good news." He caught her face with his
hands, and in the moonlight she could see his blue
eyes intently watching her. His voice dropped.
"Sandy, I love you."

"I thought you'd never tell me!" She gasped and
leaned forward, closing her eyes as he kissed her.

His arms tightened, crushing her softness to
him, and he shifted her, moving her over him on
the chaise. She raised herself. "Gabe, it's not very
private out here."

"Mmm. Let's go get a soda. Okay?"

"Isn't it kind of late?"

"No. I had a nap." He stood up and grinned, holding out his hand. How could she refuse?

In his car he pulled her close beside him, and
they rode quietly. She had the feeling she should
wait and let him talk, so she enjoyed the scent of
pine on his clothing, the warmth of his skin, the
closeness to him. They stopped in front of his
apartment.

"I thought we were going to get a soda."

"We are, at my place."

"Sure enough!"

He chuckled and held her hand while they entered his darkened apartment. He switched on a small light and turned to take her in his arms. "We have all the privacy in the world here." He ran his fingers through her hair, and pins went flying.

"I like your hair down. And now, Miss Sandy Smith, I'm going to show you how much I love you," he said huskily, and her pulse and lungs seemed to stop functioning.

"Oh, Gabe, why didn't you tell me?"

He frowned at her. "How could you not know?"

She was startled by the sincerity in his question. "We made an agreement, remember? You volunteered to date me for four weeks."

He groaned. "For a very bright person, you're dreadfully obtuse sometimes. Everything I did was because of love."

"How was I to know that? You did what you agreed to do."

"Oh, come on."

"Well, most people, when they love someone, tell that person."

"How many times did you tell me?"

She blushed. "I didn't want to tell you how much I loved you if you didn't love me in return."

"For corn's sake!" Suddenly he ran his fingers through his hair distractedly, and his voice sobered. "Pete and Jeanie are the golden children in my family. Everything is on the surface with them. They tell people they love them, they cry, they show their feelings. They're like Mom. I'm like Dad. It's all bottled up inside, and it's hard to get it out. And frankly, dear lady, I thought you knew I loved you. I really thought I acted like a man in love. But if you want to be showered with plants and teddy bears and candy—"

"Oh, my word, no! All I want is to know you love me. Just say so every now and then."

"Every now and then," he said solemnly. "I'll do that." He kissed her throat. "I love you, Sandy Smith." His lips trailed to her ear, and he kissed her. "I love you." He kissed her temple, her cheek, raining kisses to the corner of her mouth. "I love you."

She closed her eyes in bliss. "You don't have to keep on. I got the message."

"You ain't seen nothin' yet, my dear. I love you." He kissed her throat, his kisses continuing to her collarbone, while he tugged at the buttons on her dress.

Sandy relished every "I love you." She ran her hands across his shoulders in rediscovery, twisting his buttons free with shaking hands to touch his bare flesh. He inhaled deeply, making his broad chest expand. Beneath her palms she felt the pounding of his heart, which told her more than words.

The dress fell around her ankles in a cool, whispery rush. Gabe's voice was husky and rough as suddenly he faced her. "I don't intend to lose you."

Her pulse raced with joy, and her eyes felt heavy-lidded as she gazed up at him, smiling slightly. His thumbs traced the curve of her lips, starting wild tingles as she kissed his callused hand. "You won't lose me. I'm yours. My heart has been yours since that first night. Gabe—"

Her words ended as he peeled away the wisps of

nylon and picked her up in his arms to carry her to bed.

Later, she stirred, and felt his arms tighten around her. "Don't move away."

"I wouldn't think of it."

"Can you reach my trousers?"

She twisted to reach down on the floor and pick up the navy slacks. "Are you getting up?"

"Nope." He fished in a pocket and withdrew a box. "From me to you."

She sat up, shaking her hair away from her face as she took the box and looked at deep blue eyes that were filled with an unmistakable message of love. He tugged the sheet down that she had pulled over her.

She opened the box and stared at the lovely emerald-and-diamond ring.

"Will you marry me?"

She leaned down to hug him, holding him tightly as she cried.

"Hey! You're crying."

"I'm happy."

"I'm glad you told me. You and Jeanie." He laughed softly. "When you're through crying on me, will you give me an answer?"

"Of course I'll marry you."

"Ahh, here." He slipped the ring on her finger and looked at her intently. "If you don't like the emerald, we can have it changed to diamonds."

"I love the emerald."

"It reminded me of your green eyes."

"And my lovely green ginkgos. I'll love ginkgos forever."

He put his hands behind his head and gazed at her serenely. "Now, there are a few matters to get straight. You break your date for Saturday night."

"Yes, sir. I already have."

"You did? Why did you accept a date with someone else when you knew—"

"Gabe, I didn't know! I really didn't know. You never told me."

"It won't happen again."

"Promise?"

"Promise. Now, you can't move to Dallas. You know, you threw me into shock. I thought everything was fine. I loved you, I thought you loved me. I thought you knew I loved you—"

"Is there something typically male here that I might have missed?"

"Could be, although there are the males like my brother—"

"I'll settle for the strong, silent type."

"I never thought of myself as the silent type."

"Well, you are. You put me through the worst misery of my life!" She said it lightly, but he stared at her for long seconds and then pulled her down.

"I'm sorry. I'm not half so silent when I can work a nice forty-hour week and live like a normal human being."

"I know." She lay with her head on his chest, listening to his heart beat while she ran her hands over his warm flesh. His words were a grim reminder of how little time she would get to spend with him, and she sighed.

"Why the long sigh?"

"You should be asleep, because you'll be exhausted tomorrow."

He chuckled softly.

"That's the most vulgar, leering chuckle I ever heard!" She sat up in mock indignation.

"Chuckles can't leer."

"That one did."

"This is a leer." And he showed her, his gaze lowering to her full, bare breasts. She caught her breath, feeling an instant response as her breasts tightened, the nipples thrusting toward him.

His laughter died and his eyes darkened. He touched her lightly, the faintest stroke, and his voice was deep.

"You're so lovely, Sandy." He came up to touch a rosy peak with his tongue, and she gasped as hot currents shocked her.

His arms locked around her and he pulled her down, rolling her over so he was above her while he kissed her.

When dawn lightened the sky, Sandy stirred. "I have to go home."

"Why?"

"A thousand reasons. You have to go to work—"

"Wrong."

She sat up in surprise. "What?"

"Nope. I have the day off. Chad's in charge. I'm spending the day with my lady of the ginkgos."

"Who's minding the store at London and Holmes?"

"Jeanie. And it's a holiday—a long weekend, remember?"

Another surprise made her stare at him with wonder. "You put your sister in charge?"

He frowned. "What's so damned amazing about

that? Don't tell me you thought I was chauvinistic too!"

"No. I'm just surprised. She seemed so . . ."

He grinned. "So emotional—so unlike her older brother. She and Pete let it all pour out, but that doesn't mean she isn't bright and efficient. She can handle everything—frankly, as competently as Dad—if he'll just give her a chance. I'm doing it for him. This is her chance, and she's doing fine."

"How nice! How wonderful for her, for your father, for you—and for me. I'll get to see you every once in a while."

"More than that, hon. How soon can we have a wedding?"

"You'll have to wait until your folks get back from their trip."

"That's September first."

"Let's marry when the ginkgos turn gold. We can marry and have a reception outside."

"I can't wait for the ginkgos to turn gold. Do you know how long that might be?"

"How long?"

"October. Maybe the middle of September."

"You have to wait for your parents to get back. You'll be too busy until then, and Jeanie won't want you to leave for a honeymoon."

"That might be the best thing that ever happened to Jeanie."

"What about your promise to your dad that you'd take charge?"

He grinned. "I took charge and delegated authority. Dad isn't going to call until they get back to New York. You watch, she'll do a great job."

"You're a nice brother."

"I'm a very lovable guy," he said smugly, and she poked him in the ribs.

"You're so modest too!"

He laughed and pulled her down. "Let's get Gran, Dodo, and Pete and have a wedding. Work at the nursery is tapering off each day now. The big season is over. I'll delegate more to Chad."

"After all your arguments with your dad about why you couldn't leave the nursery."

He shrugged. "The nursery no longer has number-one priority."

She felt tears threaten again as she gazed into blue eyes that reinforced his statement. "You big lug . . ." she whispered softly, brushing tears away.

"When's the wedding?"

She thought about her parents, Gran, the center. "Derek has a woman who can take over here." She sat up. "I'll be unemployed, you know. I'll have to find another job, because the manager of the center has to live there. Unless you want to move into my apartment."

"And risk life and limb with Mrs. Fenster? No!"

She laughed, and he played with her hair. "Seriously, do you mind giving it up?"

"For you? You take top priority too."

"Ahhh. I want you to be happy, and you liked your job there. I hate to take that away from you."

She shrugged. "I'll find something."

"Want to work at the nursery with me? Or would you like to take classes to become a physical therapist?"

She blinked in surprise. "I don't have the money saved for that."

"Once again, I have to lay it all out for you—I'd

love to send you to college if you'd like to take the classes to become a phy—"

"Gabe, that would be grand! We'll think about it. I don't believe you should rush into something like that. It takes so much money and time. . . ."

"You might be worth it," he said lightly.

She twined her fingers in the short, soft curls on his chest. "I have to go home now."

"When is the wedding? Tomorrow?"

"Heavens, no! I can't get married tomorrow. I just find out you love me and in the next breath you want the wedding to be tomorrow."

"Right. You have that straight."

"I don't know you that well. Do you want children?"

"Yes," he answered, suddenly solemn. "And I'd bet my last dime you do too."

"You're right."

His brows drew together, and he looked away. "Sandy, there's a family secret I have to tell you."

She felt her breath catch, he looked so solemn. "What is it?"

"I'm not supposed to tell, and it may come as a terrible shock."

All sorts of things whirled through her mind— illness, inherited diseases, sterility.

"Gabe, what is it?" she asked softly.

"Pete has a new girlfriend."

It took ten seconds for her to react. "Oh, you! Do you know how much you scared me!" She pounced on him, tickling him while he laughed uproariously.

"Cut . . . it out! You can't believe how he sneaks around with her. . . . Sandy! Cut it out!" Laughter ended his words. He rolled over, knocking her flat on the mattress and pinning her hands to the bed.

"You wildcat!"

"That was tacky, tacky!"

"Mmmmm, this view isn't."

"Gabe," she whispered, instantly changing the mood. "I have to get out of bed and go home."

"Do you really?" he said, but the words were husky and seemed to come from far away, and then there were no more words at all. . . .

Epilogue

Gabe shook seeds into a sack and sealed it up, then measured out another ounce of seeds. He concentrated on what he was doing, until the faint, sweet scent of gardenias assailed him. His heart jumped, and he looked up into wide green eyes.

"It's past closing time. I hope you locked the door."

"I did. You're working late."

He glanced at his watch. "I'm sorry. We locked up at six and I started sacking up seeds and forgot the time. I'm sor—"

"Don't apologize. I was busy too."

"You haven't been here in a month."

"You know how much time my classes take."

"Come here. I want to show you something." He went around the counter and paused, wondering if he would ever tire of looking at her. It had been a year and a month since their wedding, but each time they were together his pulse jumped and he had to touch her constantly. "Sandy," he said softly, his voice dropping. He watched her green eyes darken, the lids becoming heavy in that way she had when she became passionate. His gaze lowered over her white shirt, the brown tweed skirt, her smooth, tanned legs, to her brown loafers. He inhaled deeply and pulled her to him, his lips brushing hers lightly. "My, I have a beautiful wife."

"Thank you. And I have—"

He silenced her words, kissing her until they both were breathless.

"Come here and look at this." He took her hand and led her outside.

They passed the greenhouses and went to the back, where the big trees were potted. "Look at the ginkgos."

She gasped with pleasure. "They've turned gold!"

They walked closer and looked up into two of the tallest trees. Leaves clustered like tiny golden fans, dangling overhead, and through their golden branches the October evening sky spread a scarlet blanket with the sun's last rays. "Aren't they beautiful!" she said with a gasp.

His gaze shifted from the golden leaves to her thick, silky hair. He reached out and removed a pin, then another. "So beautiful that tomorrow, two of them will be planted in our front yard."

"Oh, Gabe! How wonderful! Let's go look at our new house before we go back to the apartment."

"Sure." More pins came out, and locks tumbled over her shoulders.

"What are you doing?

"I want to look at you with your hair down."

"You can do that at home, tonight."

The last pin came out and she shook her head, long golden strands swirling over her shoulders. She raised her face and smiled. "Maybe now's a good time."

"Now's a wonderful time," he said huskily. "My golden girl beneath a golden tree—"

" 'A golden love, a part of me.' I'm quoting an old, obscure poet."

He laughed softly. "You've changed the line slightly."

She smiled and moved closer. "And soon we'll be three."

"Three!" His brows raised, and joy shook him. "You're sure?"

"No. I have an appointment to see Dr. Bates next week, and you can go with me, but I have a suspicion that all our efforts weren't in vain."

"Oh, Sandy! You don't mind giving up your classes for a time?"

"For a long time, you mean! No, I told you that. Gabe, I'm so happy."

He gave a whoop of joy and swung her into the air, holding her around the waist while her head struck a thin branch.

"Hey! Put me down!"

He lowered her into his arms as golden ginkgo leaves showered over both of them.

"Now I have leaves in my hair and so do you."

He laughed and held her, feeling as if he would burst with love. "Darling, Sandy, my sweet lady of the ginkgos, I love you."

Smiling, she wrapped her arms around his neck and pulled his mouth down to hers while more golden leaves fell unheeded over them.

THE EDITOR'S CORNER

Enthusiasm is one of the most powerful engines of success. When you do a thing, do it with your might. Put your whole soul into it. Stamp it with your own personality. Be active, be energetic, be enthusiastic and faithful, and you will accomplish your object. Nothing great was ever achieved without enthusiasm.   —Ralph Waldo Emerson

Enthusiasm is the fuel that drives the LOVESWEPT effort at Bantam Books. And our enthusiasm has never been higher for the love stories we publish than it is now in this bright new year. Our schedule for 1986 is glorious—combining the wonderful offerings of beloved favorite authors with those of exciting newcomers to romance writing. As you will see, we continue our LOVESWEPT tradition into 1986 of the marriage of something old, something new—but never something borrowed or blue!

STORM'S THUNDER, LOVESWEPT #127, by Marianne Shock is as exciting as its title suggests, while also giving us a rich, heartwarming exploration of what deep and everlasting love is all about. Patience Burke has been intrigued from afar by Storm Duchene for a very long time. When at last she meets him face-to-face, she is overwhelmed by her feelings for him—and it quickly becomes apparent that he finds her irresistible. But Storm is a man troubled by loss of a loved one and, even though he faces danger and death on the boat racing circuit, he cannot bear the thought of being bereft once more. And, so, he has decided never to love again. Yet how can he deny Patience? She may be younger and far less experienced than he, but she possesses a great deal of wisdom. She reaches out to him at just the right time and their relationship blossoms. Then, she must de-

(continued)

cide to pull away in an all-or-nothing gamble. You'll relish the warmth and wit of **STORM'S THUNDER,** and I'll bet that like me you'll be on the edge of your chair rooting for Patience as she makes her very risky, but necessary, move to win happiness with Storm.

Opening Kay Hooper's next romance for us, **REBEL WALTZ,** LOVESWEPT #128, is like stepping into a magnificent dream. Set in the South at an historic plantation house, **REBEL WALTZ** is the shimmering love story of Banner Clairmont, a gifted and beautiful young woman, who adores the mansion in which she's grown up, and dashing Rory Stewart, the sensitive and sexy man who fears he may have to take her beloved home away from her. Banner's shrewd grandfather believes at first that he is the moving force in the drama surrounding her and Rory. But very quickly he must acknowledge that it is Fate—whimsical yet certain Fate—that is working in its mysterious ways to draw this delightful couple together. Even as you close the book on **REBEL WALTZ,** its magic will linger, leaving you with the rosy glow and warmth of a lovely dream.

I think all of us true romantics believe that love knows no boundaries of age or position in society. And I also think you'll agree with me that no one could better explore that proposition in a delightful love story than our own Billie Green. In **MRS. GALLAGHER AND THE NE'ER DO WELL,** LOVESWEPT #129, Billie gives us two outwardly different people who have all the most important things in common. Helen Gallagher is a charming widow of some standing in her community; Tom Peters is a free-spirit, a bold vagabond who yearns to take her away from her small town and constricted way of life into a world of romance and adventure. Helen cannot resist the delightful rogue . . . nor can she turn aside the pressures to live out the roles of mother and citizen for which she's

(continued)

been reared. You'll thrill to Helen's discovery of her true self (with the best kind of help from Tom!) . . . as you keep your fingers crossed for her to find the courage to follow her heart. A truly unforgettable love story!

Several years ago I had the rewarding experience of reading several emotionally touching romances by Patt Bucheister, writing under a pen name. Now we're pleased that she has become a LOVESWEPT author—writing under her real name, of course—with **NIGHT AND DAY,** LOVESWEPT #130. Patt's hero, Cole Denver, is a perplexing man whose enigmatic personality just about drives heroine Chalis Quinn over the edge. By day he is curt, withdrawn, a sort of silent and distant macho man. By night he is charming, tender, almost a dream lover. What accounts for the changes in Cole? Why—when there is such caring and passion between them—doesn't he let Chalis into his life by day, as well as night? Getting the answers to those questions isn't half so difficult as knowing what to *do* with them! But Chalis is as spunky as she is sensitive and determines that with her help love will find a way. We hope you will enjoy this humorous and moving love story and give Patt a warm welcome.

Warm wishes,

Sincerely,

Carolyn Nichols

Carolyn Nichols
  Editor
LOVESWEPT
Bantam Books, Inc.
666 Fifth Avenue
New York, NY 10103